I0619583

Firestar

The Dragon Star Chronicles, Volume 1

Olivia Gold

Published by Olivia Gold, 2025.

Cover designed and illustrated by Eliora Humphrey (@eliora_doesart)

Published by Olivia Gold

ISBNs:

Paperback: 9798991937740

Ebook: 9798991937757

Table of Contents

For Jude and Riley

Author's Note

This is my first time writing a middle-grade fantasy story, and I truly had so much fun working on this project. This story features a character who was born hearing but has lost his hearing over time. This was a challenge for me to write, ensuring that I portrayed his deafness well through my words. Aidan quickly became one of my favorite characters in the story, and I hope I did his character justice.

While I realize that in ASL, signs are not used for every word "spoken" when communicating, for the sake of simplicity for my younger readers (specifically for ages 8-12), I chose to write in complete word-for-word signs. I hope this upholds the integrity of the story and also honors my deaf character, Aidan.

I hope you love this story as much as I do and that you enjoy getting lost in the Kingdom of Kida with Aidan, Leola, Enya, and Seraphina.

Chapter 1

How Legends Begin

Seraphina dreamed about the impossible at least three times a day, and she desperately needed her sister to believe in it as well. Enya never took her interests seriously, but she wanted her big sister to come with her to the cove nonetheless. Of course, Enya was always preoccupied, lost with her head in a scroll.

The cove offered the most amazing views of the stars when the sun set for the day, and the two moons rose in its place. Since it was the first clear night in two weeks, tonight was perfect for spying the dragon constellations through the cove's window to the sky. The spring clouds and storms had kept the stars hidden for long enough, but tonight—tonight it was perfect. It was the start of summer and a break from their normal study season.

"Enya, please! I want to see the dragons. Mom and Dad already said we could go." Seraphina tugged on Enya's tunic a little more forcefully this time.

"Sera, stop. I told you I'm not done yet." Enya shrugged out of her sister's grasp and went back to poring over her parchment again.

"Enya, this isn't fair. I can't go without you, and you're always reading. Can't you take a break for a little bit?"

Seraphina tried to make her eyes look big. She tried to look as sweet as possible. Enya didn't even turn her head toward her.

It was time for a different approach.

"Well...Leola and Aidan were going to come, too, you know. They'll probably be here any minute." She singsonged.

If there was one thing that Enya hated, it was being left out. Like any good sister, Seraphina used this to her advantage without remorse.

Enya dropped her head into her hands before rolling up the parchment and letting out a deep sigh.

"Okay, Sera, let's go. But only because I want to ask Leola about something from our studies from the last session."

Seraphina rolled her eyes at her big sister, but she knew better than to speak anything negative about studies. All children in the kingdom of Kida were required to attend studies from the age of seven until they were seventeen. Lessons on reading, the history of Kida, mathematics, and preservation of growing things were interesting, but Seraphina didn't care for them as much as Enya did. Seraphina's favorite subject was also the one given the least amount of study time. A History of Dragons always fascinated her, but of course, they only spent one year studying that at age eight, and Seraphina would miss attending that particular study now that she was nine. Enya didn't think studying legends was important, but she didn't care what Enya thought, and dragons were her favorite creature to have ever existed.

"Enya! Sera! Your friends are here!" Mom called from the bottom of the ladder that led up to their shared loft.

Enya jumped up and hurried to the ladder with Seraphina following close behind. How they both managed to make it down without falling was nothing short of miraculous.

"Slow down, girls." Their father warned.

Both girls straightened their tunics and tried their best not to shove past each other to be the first to greet their friends. Enya managed to slip ahead of Seraphina at the last moment and stepped into the front room ahead of her.

Waiting next to the door were Leola and her brother Aidan. Aidan smiled when he spotted the sisters.

"Hi, are you ready to go to the cove?" He signed.

Seraphina pushed past Enya and signed while speaking aloud in response. "Yes, I am! Enya is taking forever to get ready, though, because all she wants to do is study."

"Hey, that's not true," Enya argued.

Seraphina rolled her eyes, and Aidan laughed. Enya started asking Leola about something from their studies while she put on her cloak. Seraphina moved closer to Aidan, remaining silent this time while she signed.

"Did I sign that right?" She took her time making the motions with her hands and fingers. She was still insecure about her ability to speak with her hands and was worried she had messed up.

Aidan grabbed her hands, slowed down the motions, and repeated what she had first said to him when she greeted him. She narrowed her eyes, observing intensely, then tried again. He smiled and nodded.

Aidan had slowly lost his hearing as he got older. One moment, he heard just fine (at least that's what Sera thought to be true), and the next, his hearing faded away. His parents worked hard to help him communicate in the language of hands. For the past two years, Enya and Seraphina, along with their parents, spent time practicing the same language with an elder in their village who also taught Aidan and his family. All village elders spoke with both their hands and their mouths, and many others used both languages to communicate as well.

Aidan was Seraphina's best friend, and she decided she would practice as much as possible to communicate the easiest way for Aidan.

"Are you two coming?" Leola asked from the open door, waving her hand near Aidan's face to get his attention. Aidan and Sera looked at each other and smiled before hurrying out the door after their siblings.

"How many dragon constellations do you think we'll find tonight?" Sera asked Leola.

"I'm not sure. We might just find one or two. The sky hasn't been clear in so long, and the stars don't shine with the same brightness every night." Aidan's sister answered.

"I'm so excited. I hope we find at least five!"

"Five seems a bit ambitious, Sera."

"Enni, I wasn't asking you."

Enya huffed and picked up her pace, with Leola hurrying to keep up. Sera's shoulders sagged, and her heart gave a tiny twinge of pain. Lately, she and Enya seemed to be at odds. Things had started changing between them, and she wasn't sure if it was because of her or because Enya was getting older and showing interest in more grown-up things.

Aidan tapped her shoulder, drawing her attention back to him. It was dark now, and she knew he wouldn't try to sign. Instead, he slipped his hand into hers and squeezed reassuringly. They walked like that, and it was nice to feel like someone still saw her when others moved on.

The path sloped downward, and the forest reached its branches into the road, forcing them all to walk directly down the middle. The night air was cool, but not cold, and Kida's two moons were in their sleeping phase and were much dimmer than when they were full.

Crickets chirped, and the occasional owl hooted, but no other villagers walked the road. There may be some in the cove already, but most would be settling into their homes for the night, content to rest and enjoy the quiet that the stormless night offered.

When the road leveled out again, the group turned to the left, where a narrow trail cut through the thick trees. It was well-worn, kept clean by the countless number of visitors who passed through it to enter the cove. The tiny village of Ebonfore was nestled in the thickest forest in the kingdom. It provided the kingdom with lumber and herbal medicines, and it imported most of its vegetables. While some berries and fruit trees existed within the confines of the forest, bread and vegetables were hard to come by.

The only place in the entire village where one could see the sky unobstructed was the cove, which was why Seraphina had been begging to go all day. She loved the stars, and she loved dragons. The possibility of sighting the dragon stars was the best of both worlds.

They walked single file along the path until it opened into a beautiful meadow with a gurgling stream cutting through the middle. A few torches proved they were not the only ones coming to the cove tonight.

Seraphina released Aidan's hand and ran into the open space, smiling up at the sky. Even Enya and Leola couldn't help but marvel at the beauty of it. Stars sparkled across the span of it, and the picture was exactly what Sera wanted it to be—dazzling.

A few of the village elders greeted them before resuming their study of the stars.

"It's amazing!" She was in heaven. She plopped down on the ground and fell back into the dew-damp grass, staring up at the stars above.

Enya and Leola sat next to each other to her right, and Aidan joined her on his back to her left. For several long moments, they all gazed at the sky. It was beautiful—seeing stars after so many days of only clouds.

Sera searched for a dragon constellation, hoping she would finally spot one. They were rare stars, and they moved and shifted wherever they wanted to. Sometimes, they gathered together. Other times, they stayed so far apart that no shape could form out of the clusters.

"Do you see one?" Enya whispered to Leola.

"No, not yet. We could ask an elder if they've spotted any."

Sera tugged on Aidan's cloak, getting his attention. The yellow glow of nearby torches offered barely enough light to see. She signed and spoke, "Do you think we'll see any?"

He looked to the sky again, scanning from left to right. Turning his face back to her, he looked uncertain and shrugged.

She sighed and resumed her search.

A burst of excited voices broke the silence of the cove, and three of the kids turned to find a few elders clustered together, pointing toward one particular spot. Sera tugged on Aidan's sleeve and pointed toward the adults. All four children focused on the heavens and scoured the sky in the area that had captured the elders' attention.

"There! There it is!" Enya pointed to the sky toward a small cluster of red-tinted stars.

"Oh! I see it too! That's amazing! I can't believe we're actually seeing a dragon constellation." Leola and Enya jumped to their feet and trotted toward the elders.

Sera kept searching, trying desperately to get her eyes to see what the others so quickly identified. The stars were all blending, and she felt more and more upset with each passing minute. A tug on her sleeve drew her attention away from the glittery sky.

Aidan smiled, signing, "Breathe, Sera. It's okay. See? Look right there." He tugged her closer to his side, pointing to an area of the sky farther east.

There it was! She could finally see the constellation. The stars had a reddish hue, and they formed an outline of a dragon in flight. Sera gasped, her heart growing light at the beauty of the image.

Suddenly, excited whispers filled the air once more. Everyone pointed to another spot. One elder pointed to the west, another to the north. Aidan gasped, jumping to his feet and tugging Sera up with him. She realized what the excitement was all about.

The sky was full of dragon stars! Not one, not two, but four dragon constellations filled the night sky. Sera and Aidan hurried to where Enya and Leola were standing near the elders.

Never had so many of them appeared in the sky at once. It was a miracle, or maybe it was a sign.

Seraphina blocked out the voices of the adults, her sister, and her friends. Whatever it meant, it must be something amazing. She couldn't wait to tell her parents about it when they got home.

Yes, something magical was coming. She could feel it.

Chapter 2

The Mysterious Echo

The next few days passed in a blur of excitement and wonder. Everyone in the village was talking about the stars and what they meant. When dragons roamed the world, magic flowed freely through all living things. From the smallest plant to the highest mountain—everything carried a trace of magic within it.

However, dragons have been gone for hundreds of years, and the world is a bit more restless because of it. Storms happen all the time, and droughts plague other areas of the continent. With the arrival of an abundance of dragon stars, many wondered if magic might be waking up again.

"I can't believe we saw four dragon stars! They were so beautiful." Sera nudged Enya again. "Are you listening, Enya? Do you think we'll see more soon?"

Enya rolled her eyes. "Not likely. It's been storming for the past two days. Who knows when we'll see the sky again?"

Disappointment roiled in Sera's stomach. The stars were important. She knew they were, and she couldn't help the excitement that filled her chest every time she thought about it. Enya was back to focusing only on her studies, though, leaving Sera to dream alone.

"I'm gonna go ask Mom and Dad if I can visit Aidan." She waited to see if Enya would show any sign of wanting to join her.

Her sister waved her hand and said, "Whatever."

Sera scurried down the ladder of the loft and into the kitchen, searching for one of her parents. Her father stood at the stove, stirring something in a large soup pot. His dark skin glistened with sweat. He must have recently come in from the forest and taken over the cooking for their mother.

"Dad, where is Mom?"

He started at the sound of her voice and laughed. "Sorry, Ser, I didn't hear you come down. Mom just took some soup to the neighbors. One of the little ones is sick again."

More sickness. More storms. Something was definitely not right.

"When do you think she'll be back?" She slid her foot back and forth on the floor, twisting her fingers together.

Her dad narrowed his eyes at her. "Not sure. But I can probably help you with whatever you need."

She shrugged and walked to the window. "No, that's okay. I don't need anything."

"You sure?"

"Yeah." She rested her elbows on the windowsill and stared into the darkening night.

It wasn't long before Mom walked in through the front door and pulled her damp cloak off, hanging it on the hook on the wall.

"Yuck, it's getting nasty out there. It's no wonder Constance is sick again."

Seraphina ran, throwing herself into her mom's warm arms.

"Well, what's the occasion for this?"

"No reason." Dad followed and gave his wife a peck on the cheek.

"Well, I'll happily accept it. Did you stir the soup like I asked?"

"Of course, I did, love."

"And did you not steal any bites of it either?"

Dad smiled sheepishly, "Of course I did."

She swatted him, but Sera couldn't wait another moment.

"Mom, can I go to Aidan's house?"

Dad threw his hands up in disbelief. "Why didn't you ask me!?"

Sera shrugged and kept her eyes on Mom's face.

Mom laughed, "I don't see why you can't. Just be home quickly. It's raining again."

She didn't wait for them to change their minds. She snatched her cloak from the hook, tying it quickly and shoving her feet into her still-damp boots.

Closing the door behind her, she ran down the path toward Aidan's house. The sky darkened more as thicker clouds moved overhead. A steady drizzle wet her cheeks, and she pulled her hood up, trying to keep her hair as dry as possible. Her mom had recently braided her and Enya's hair, and she didn't want to ruin it so soon after it had been done.

The path inclined as she hurried toward the village center. The trees' branches hung heavy over the trail, weighed down by the water on their leaves. It made the path appear darker than usual, and her heart skipped a beat as the shadows stretched overhead.

She slowed to a brisk walk to avoid tripping over any roots or branches that may have been marring the path. It wouldn't be long now. She was almost there. She simply had to get past the cave entrance along the mountain, and Aidan's home wasn't far beyond that.

As she crept close to the cave, the shadows seemed to reach for her. A strange heaviness filled the air, and she did her best to hug the side of the path farther from the cave's entrance. The moment she stepped in line with the large opening, a tingling sensation ran down her arms, covering them in goosebumps.

What was that?

She knew she shouldn't, but she froze and stared into the darkness of the cave. Did she hear a sound? Or was she imagining things?

She shifted her weight from one foot to the other before dragging her eyes away from the opening. But the moment she took a step, the strange feeling returned. A soft screech echoed from the cave. The sound made her heart pound. She wanted to move. She wanted to leave, but a part of her couldn't ignore the sound.

The screech echoed again, and she knew in that moment she couldn't turn back. Her feet moved on their own, carrying her to the cave and whatever hid within.

Chapter 3

Surprising Encounters

She tiptoed cautiously toward the cave entrance. A part of her knew she should turn around and keep walking to Aidan's house, but the strangeness of the cave called to her, drawing her to its yawning mouth. Her toe bumped into a rock at the entrance, clattering ahead of her into the shadows. She paused, waiting for something to respond or react to her intrusion.

The soft screech echoed from the depths of the cave again. Taking a deep breath and wiping her hands quickly on her cloak, she forced herself to move into the shadows. She didn't think about bringing a torch. It was getting darker, but it wasn't quite sunset yet. The cave didn't care. It shunned light and beckoned her into it, the mildewy scent of earth and moisture welcoming her. She wrinkled her nose at the smell, but she refused to let it stop her.

Something waited in the darkness of the cave, and for some strange reason, she was meant to find it.

"I can do this," she whispered. "It's just a normal cave."

She reached a hand outward as she crept toward the edge of the cave, trying to feel the cool stone of the wall. When her fingers made contact, she used the wall to guide her along, deeper into the heart of the cave.

A steady rhythm thrummed through her fingers where she touched the wall. It reminded her of the drums used at sacred ceremonies to Jadon, the god of their world, when they gathered with the other villagers. The soft pulse made her fingertips tingle, and she suppressed a giggle she knew she shouldn't let out. Whatever was in the cave, she didn't want to scare it or surprise it with her presence.

Screech.

The sound came louder this time, and Sera's heart beat faster in response. She blinked her eyes like that would help her see better in the black of the cave. Of course, it didn't help at all, and for the first time, she wondered if this might be a bad idea.

She should leave—go find Aidan and maybe come back with a torch to make it easier to maneuver—but before she could turn around, her hand slipped off the wall, making her stumble. She hadn't realized the cave turned toward her right, and as she peeked around the corner, a soft green glow lit the inner chamber.

She gasped, covering her mouth with her hand to silence herself. Now that she could see clearly, the path was easier to walk along. She crept slowly into the chamber and toward the strange, large rock at its center. The pulsing she had felt through the wall was coming from the stone. She could see the rock vibrate with every beat. The green light spread outward, filling the chamber with a strange, otherworldly appearance.

Another soft screech resonated through the cave, echoing off the walls. The sound came from the stone. As she neared it, the light revealed movement deep within it. It wasn't a stone at all; it was an egg! A mixture of terror and excitement rushed through her body. This egg was huge. Where did it come from, and how did it get here? It was twice as tall as her. What could possibly be inside it?

She had to tell someone. Reaching her hand forward, she pressed her fingertips onto the shell. It was warm, almost hot, and vibrating with every beat of the heart of whatever creature was waiting to emerge from its protection.

A screech pulsed outward louder this time. Whatever moved inside seemed to shift toward her hand. It pressed against the surface, and the tiniest crack fractured beneath her palm. She yanked her hand back and turned to run out of the cave. She had to find Aidan, to show him what she'd discovered! Maybe Leola would come, too.

She hurried out of the cave, tripping over her feet in her rush, but she didn't hesitate. Heading in the direction of Aidan's house, Seraphina couldn't hide the smile spreading across her face.

She spotted his house farther down the path, and her pace quickened. Aidan and Leola's dad, Milo, stepped out of the door the moment Sera ran up.

"Whoa! Sera, what's the rush?"

She skidded to a stop, doing everything in her power to control her breathing and racing heart.

"I'm sorry! I really, really need to talk to Aidan right now."

Milo chuckled before stepping aside and gesturing toward the door in invitation. She didn't wait for him to ask any other questions.

When she burst into their house, she headed straight for the back, where Aidan's and Leola's rooms were. Leola started at the sudden intrusion, but Aidan continued to tinker with a new creation of his with his back toward the door.

"Seraphina, what are you doing here? It's kinda late, isn't it?" Leola reached over from her spot on Aidan's bed and tapped him on the shoulder, drawing his attention to the door.

Sera paused, feeling unsure about whether she should tell Leola about the egg in the cave, too. Aidan smiled before signing.

"Are you okay? You look a little...pukey."

Sera wrinkled her nose and shook her head in confusion. "I don't look..." She paused, waving her hands around as if that would help her sign the right thing better.

"He said you look sweaty, Sera. No need to get so upset." Leola laughed.

"Oh." Sera felt her cheeks warm in embarrassment as she offered a shy smile before continuing. "I'm still getting confused about some of the signs."

Aidan waved his hand dismissively. "No big deal. You'll learn them eventually. Now what's up?"

She eyed Leola warily before answering. "I found something."

Aidan's eyes widened, but it was Leola who responded first. "What are you talking about?"

"Exactly, that. I. Found. Something. It's in a cave, and I think you should see it."

"In the cave? Cool! Want to go, Le?" Aidan was already standing and setting down the tools he was using.

"I don't know. It's getting kind of late. What exactly did you find in a cave, Sera?"

Sera took a deep breath before answering. "I think it's an egg."

Chapter 4

Discovery

Aidan stared at Seraphina with his mouth agape.

"An egg?" He signed.

The excitement on Sera's face said she believed what she said was true, but what was so special about an egg, anyway? Leola looked as doubtful as he felt.

"Yes, an egg! Just come and see, okay? I promise, you won't regret it. It's too hard to explain without showing you." She gestured to the door and started to move.

Aidan figured it wouldn't hurt to see for himself. He jumped up to follow, with Leola close on his heels.

"What were you doing in a cave, Sera? Seems like a strange place to explore by yourself," Leola said as she and Aidan grabbed their cloaks from their hooks.

Sera was jittery now, impatient and eager for them to get going. "It was weird. I was on my way to find you, Aidan, when I heard a strange screeching sound. It's like something called me. When I went to see what it was, I found an egg with a strange green light coming off it."

They all stepped out of the house and into a steady drizzle of rain. The clouds had finally burst open, and everything grew darker and more ominous. Pulling their hoods up, they hurried down the path following closely behind Sera as she led the way to the cave.

As they drew near the cave entrance, the air around them changed. Aidan could feel it, and he could tell Leola did too. They exchanged a glance, silently acknowledging the shift in their surroundings. Their bodies hummed with a strange vibration, syncing with their heartbeats and pulsing through them.

Aidan reached forward, grabbing Sera by the shoulder to gain her attention. When she faced him, he signed, "Are you sure about this? Something feels weird about this place."

She responded, "Yes! Just trust me." And with that, she stepped into the darkness of the cave.

Aidan and Leola stared after her for only a moment before following her inside.

"Sera, wait up!" Leola slid in front of Aidan, shielding him from whatever was waiting for them.

They ran their hands along the cool stone walls and followed the steady footsteps of Sera ahead of them. When the wall shifted away from them, they turned the corner and squinted their eyes against the brightness of a strange glowing light.

Leola opened her mouth in a gasp while Sera turned her gaze back to her friends, a satisfied smile on her face. The strange stone gave off just enough light for Aidan to see Sera sign to him.

"I told you it was cool."

He nodded, stunned, his mouth slightly open in awe. He moved closer, and suddenly, he realized why Sera thought it was an egg. The light within the stone pulsed a steady *thump-thump,* just like a heartbeat. He wondered if a sound coincided with the light's movement. He turned to see what Leola might do.

She shuffled closer to the stone before voicing her reaction.

"Is that a heartbeat? Inside the stone?"

Sera smiled. "I think it is."

"What would lay an egg that looks like a stone? And why is the light coming from it blue?"

Sera's brow furrowed. "The light isn't blue. It's green."

Leola shook her head. "No, I see a blue light."

Aidan waved his hands to grab their attention.

"I see a red light, though," he signed.

Confusion filled their faces. They each saw a different light, but why?

Leola straightened her shoulders before responding. "Well, this is weird and possibly dangerous. Where is Enya? We should go get her."

Sera's face dropped, disappointed at the lack of excitement coming from Leola. She lifted her eyes to Aidan, hope brimming inside their depths.

"She wasn't with me when I came by here. I came to your house first." Her signing was a bit sloppy, revealing just how much her friends' responses had impacted her. Aidan squinted his eyes and stepped closer to her, grabbing her hands. He gestured for her to repeat herself.

When she did, he smiled and nudged Leola.

"You should go get her. Bring her here, and we can see what she thinks. She loves to study scrolls as much as you do. Maybe she'll have some ideas."

Leola frowned, "I don't want to leave you guys here alone."

"We'll be fine! The egg looks the same as it did when I first found it. Please go get Enya." Sera pleaded.

The eagerness in Sera's eyes was all Leola needed to see. "Okay, but you better not touch that thing while I'm gone. Be safe! Okay?" She signed the last part with emphasis, and Aidan and Sera nodded their agreement vigorously.

Turning to leave, Leola moved cautiously along the wall until she slipped around the corner and slipped out of sight.

Aidan smirked toward Sera before moving toward the stone or egg or whatever this thing was. Sera's eyes widened, but she didn't stop him.

As he drew closer, the pulses strengthened enough that he could feel the rhythm in his chest, and a strange pressure built in his ears. Sera came up beside him when he hesitated inches away from the stone. Reaching down, she took his hand in hers, and he knew, then, that he needed to do this. He understood what she meant by being drawn to the cave, to the force hiding within it.

They shared a look, and she nodded her agreement.

He reached his other hand slowly toward the red light emanating from the stone. He expected the surface to be cold like the cave walls. Maybe even feel a bit damp. Instead, it was warm, almost hot to the touch.

The light grew brighter, responding to him, and both he and Sera closed their eyes against the intensity of it. The egg trembled beneath his hands, and he felt a rumble emit from deep inside it. Then, with his eyes still closed, the pulsing heartbeat within slowed, and his ears rang.

He wanted to pull away—to let go and flee the cave. Sera tugged on his hand, and he imagined she must be saying something to him that he couldn't hear. But as quickly as the light grew, it dimmed, and he felt the stone beneath his fingers settle.

He was about to move his hand away when something stirred under his palm, and a voice reached his normally silent ears.

What is your name, Firestar?

Chapter 5

Revelation

Aidan snatched his hand back and stumbled over his feet before falling to the ground. Sera squealed and rushed to Aidan's side, grabbing under his arm to help him to his feet. He felt shaky under her grip.

He remained transfixed on the egg, and she had to force his gaze toward her.

"What happened? Are you okay?" Her fingers felt awkward as she signed hastily, but Aidan understood well enough.

He blinked his eyes slowly and nodded, but his gaze remained unfocused. She shook his shoulders and waved a hand in front of him again. Whatever had happened when he touched the egg had left him deeply bothered. He pulled his attention from the stone and zeroed in on Sera. She repeated her question.

He signed, "I—heard something."

Sera's brow furrowed in confusion. "What do you mean you heard something? Did you feel something shake?"

He shook his head firmly. "No, no, I *heard* something. When I touched the surface, something spoke to me."

Chills ran up Sera's arms. That wasn't possible. Aidan hadn't heard anything in over a year.

"What did it say?" She had to know. This was magic, plain and simple—it had to be.

"It asked me my name?" He paused, lowering his hands slowly. He stepped toward the egg again and lifted his hands cautiously.

Before he made contact, voices rang through the cavern, and Sera grabbed his arms. He shot her an annoyed look before seeing her point back toward the cave opening.

Leola and Enya crept into the tight space, pausing when they saw how close the others were to the egg.

"What are you doing? I told you to be careful!" Leola signed as she stomped toward her brother.

"Wait!" Sera pressed her hands out to stop Leola's approach. Enya stepped up behind Leola, peering around her in wonder at the glowing object.

"Sera, move," Leola ground out.

"You don't understand. Aidan experienced something amazing!" Sera's eyes lit up with excitement at the discovery.

Aidan gestured wildly at them both, then made tight fists in front of himself.

"I'm sorry, Aidan." Leola signed as she spoke. "I got carried away."

"Yeah, me too. Sorry." Sera's cheeks flushed with embarrassment before she repeated what she said with her hands, too.

"Aidan experienced something amazing."

"What do you mean?" Enya asked without taking her eyes off the egg.

"I heard something when I touched it," Aidan answered.

Confusion coated the others' faces.

"You... heard something?"

Sera understood Leola's disbelief, but another emotion mingled with that one on her face—fear. Why would Leola find this scary?

"Isn't that amazing?" She asked, trying to get Leola to see the beauty of this moment.

Instead, Leola pulled her brother farther away from the strange egg.

"This isn't right. I don't think we should stay here. We should tell someone. An elder, maybe." Leola tried to shuffle backwards, but Aidan yanked his arm free.

"NO! I'm not leaving. I heard something, Le! I have to see. What if..." He didn't finish his thought.

Enya stepped forward. "What did it say to you, whatever this voice was that you heard? And what about you, Sera? Did you hear it speak to Aidan?"

Sera opened her mouth to answer, then felt bashful at the truth. "I didn't hear anything. But I wasn't touching it. Aidan was. Maybe that's why he heard something." She stared at her feet, nudging some rocks out of her path to give herself something to do.

"I still can't believe you touched it." Leola ground out.

"Well, I did. It said, 'What is your name, Firestar?'"

"Firestar?" Enya signed slowly. "Are you sure that's what it said?"

Sera's eyes flicked to Aidan's. A strange feeling filled her chest at the mention of the name. It felt important. She'd never heard the term, but it stirred something inside of her.

"Yes! That's what it said." Aidan turned his attention back toward the egg. The light emanating from it glowed a different shade for each of them when they had first arrived. But now, all they could see was red.

"We can't tell anyone about this. They'll be afraid." Sera knew this with certainty, though she couldn't explain why. This was a sacred thing, and though her people found the dragon stars to be wondrous and signs important enough to seek out, they did not speak of dragons as something safe, and it must be a dragon's egg, right? What else could it be?

Maybe if she touched it, a voice would speak to her as well. Without hesitating, she surged toward the glowing stone and held her hands out.

"Sera! What are you doing?" Enya lunged after her but missed.

When her hands collided with the rough surface, she noticed warmth and vibrations coming from within. She waited, hoping, praying she would hear something special too. All that met her was silence.

Disappointment hung heavy on her shoulders.

Aidan scooted up next to her and placed a gentle hand on her shoulder. She let hers drop and focused her gaze on him.

"Did you hear anything?"

She shook her head solemnly.

"Maybe you should try again, Aidan."

"I think that's a bad idea. Please come with me." Leola tried to grab Aidan—to drag him home, where it was safe, where nothing strange or mysterious could happen to her little brother, but Aidan held a firm hand up, signaling no.

Then, he placed his hands on the egg again.

Why did you run from me, Firestar?

Aidan wasn't sure how he should try to communicate with whatever was in the egg. He didn't think speaking with his hands would work because whatever was in the egg couldn't see him. He decided to try pushing a thought toward whatever was hidden within and hope for the best.

I...I don't think I'm who you are hoping I will be.

You are whoever you think you are. He heard it. He couldn't believe it had actually worked! Whatever was in the egg had heard him and responded to him through his mind—a voice, speaking to him for the first time in a long time.

What does Firestar mean? Maybe he could get a proper answer.

That is for me to know and you to earn. Or maybe not.

He wanted to ask what the strange being was, but he thought that might be rude. Instead, he asked for its name.

My name is also for me to know, and for you to earn.

He was about to ask another question when Leola yanked him back hard enough that he would have fallen had she not kept a firm hold on his arms.

"That's enough. We're leaving."

Sera and Aidan both protested.

"No, Leola's right. We need to think about this. We need to discuss what the best thing to do is," Enya reasoned.

"The best thing to do is get an elder," Leola huffed.

"I'm not sure. Let's sleep on it and meet back here tomorrow when it's daytime. It's too dark now, and our parents will be wondering where we are."

Enya eyed Sera, and Sera nodded in agreement, relief flooding her veins that, for once, her sister had sided with her.

Leola sighed, "Okay. Let's meet here at first light. Don't go in alone." She emphasized this last part, staring daggers at both Aidan and Sera.

They all agreed and soon ventured out onto the shadowy forest path. Aidan felt certain that a pulse of energy had reached out toward him as he'd walked away. Whatever was in the egg had chosen him, and he wasn't sure why. But he was determined to find out.

Chapter 6

The Things We Miss

Aidan tossed and turned all night long. Leola heard his restlessness and found herself getting anxious with each passing moment. When she finally jostled him awake, the sky was transitioning from dark blue to gray, and he seemed more than ready to confront whatever waited for them inside the cave.

"Are you ready?" Leola signed.

Worry tightened her throat. She spent most of the night searching through their scrolls for anything that had to do with dragons. Their parents asked at one point what she was up to, and she'd told them she had an interesting side project she wanted to research, but she couldn't bring herself to ask them any questions about dragons.

Aidan nodded and pulled his cloak from the peg by the front door.

"We're going out to meet with Enya and Seraphina. We have a surprise we're working on." Leola told their mother.

"It's awfully early to be heading out. Why the rush? I haven't even made breakfast yet."

"We need the perfect lighting. We want to catch the sunrise at just the right moment." She rushed her words, pleading with the god, Jadon, for favor.

Their mother narrowed her eyes. "Okay. But be careful. Don't wander into the forest, and please stay on the trail."

Brother and sister nodded earnestly before dashing through the door. They remained silent on the trip toward the cave until Leola stopped Aidan with a hand to his shoulder.

"I don't want you to touch that thing again."

Aidan's face scrunched in frustration. "I want to know why I can hear it. Don't you want to find answers? What if..." He paused, wrestling with the question he wanted to ask. "What if it can give me my hearing back?"

He hoped she would agree with him, but when she stayed quiet, he fled, leaving her behind with a heavy feeling in her chest. She couldn't say what he wanted her to, but as he stomped down the trail, his hands clenched into fists at his sides, she regretted her silence.

Leola's belly tightened in anxiety. Hope was a dangerous thing. She kept her thoughts to herself and followed after him. Soon, quiet chatter up ahead drew her attention, and she spotted Enya and Sera standing outside the cave entrance.

Aidan rushed up to Sera, signing excitedly about what they might discover, but Leola sought Enya's eyes. Her friend watched her curiously, perhaps understanding just how scared she was.

"Are you ready?" Enya asked.

Leola shrugged, "As ready as I'll ever be." She dropped her voice down a notch, "I just don't want him to get hurt."

Enya smiled sadly, "I know. But maybe something good will come out of it."

She didn't think so, but she didn't feel like arguing either.

"Okay," Enya touched Sera's arm. "It's time to give this another shot. Are you ready?"

All four of them nodded before Enya stepped to the front and walked into the cave. The inside was damp this morning, more than it had been the night before. The coolness at the entrance gave way to a strange warmth the farther in they went. Leola's heart pounded. The egg must be giving off heat. Did they need any other confirmation that a dragon waited inside it?

Enya stumbled slightly as she approached the bend, and a light glow filled the space ahead. Leola reached out to place one hand on the cave wall and another on Enya's shoulder. She felt her friend draw in a deep breath before continuing. Perhaps she wasn't the only one nervous about what may be waiting for them.

When they turned the corner, a collective gasp escaped all four friends. A bright white light filled the cavern, and the heat coming from it made them sweaty.

"What's happening? I can't see!" Seraphina's voice filled the chamber, and the egg trembled in response. Whatever was inside knew they had arrived.

"It's too bright and too hot! Maybe we should leave?" Enya answered.

Leola wanted to agree, but she felt her brother's hands reach out and press into her back. He pressed on her to shift her to the side, making an effort to get around her. She reached back to grab his hand, squeezing it in a silent plea. It was so bright she could barely keep her eyes open a crack.

"I think we should go." Leola agreed with Enya.

"No! Something's happening. We need to stay." Sera demanded.

Leola was about to speak again when she heard her brother gasp. He had managed to squirm past her and step toward the egg.

"No, don't go over there, Aidan! Please!" But he couldn't hear her, and he couldn't see her hands. She shuffled forward past Enya and Sera and reached toward Aidan's back when the light vanished, plunging them into darkness.

The black filling the space now was so intense. Little splashes of light filled her vision for a moment. Humming swelled around them; a rhythm felt deep in their chests.

"Aidan?" Leola didn't know why she was speaking aloud, but her brain had reverted to the past, and she couldn't stop herself.

She shuffled forward until she felt his back. She knew without seeing that he was touching the egg. Nothing terrible had happened yet, but that didn't mean it was safe.

Aiden's breathing was rapid, and before she could react, he snatched her hand and pressed it to the egg. A squeal escaped her lips, but he pressed his hand firmly against hers until she calmed. The egg felt like stone, and warmth seeped out of it into her palm.

A soft red glow filled the room, and something shifted against the hard shell. She drew back, afraid of the unknown waiting inside.

Aidan tapped her shoulder, forcing her eyes to his. "Did you feel it?"

She nodded, mouth open.

"Wow, it's beautiful." Sera moved to stand next to the others, followed closely by Enya.

"What did you feel?" Enya asked.

"Something moved beneath my hand." Leola trembled, her voice as unsteady as her body.

"I told you this was important," Aidan signed.

She couldn't disagree. Sera stretched her hand toward the egg when a crack formed on the surface.

"Don't touch it!" Enya yanked Sera back, and Leola followed close behind.

The soft red glow intensified. She was mesmerized by the breaks forming quickly over the surface of the egg and didn't realize that Aidan hadn't moved away.

Leola surged forward, desperate to reach him before whatever was waking up did. The heat in the chamber intensified, and the light grew in strength, forcing her to squint. She stumbled, and when she thought she'd made it, the ground rumbled with power, sending her to her knees. Sera and Enya cried out, and Leola watched in horror as Aidan fell forward toward the egg.

The outer shell gave way, sending streams of light and heat outward. Aidan vanished within the brightness, and Leola screamed.

Moments later, the light dulled, and the ground stilled. Shouts of concern crept into the cave, bouncing off the walls. Others felt the earthquake as well. People frantically called to one another, taking a count of all members of their community. It wouldn't be long before the four of them were discovered missing.

Leola wiped dust from her eyes and leaped to her feet. Aidan knelt on the ground before the cracked egg, staring, stunned at what lay amidst the shards.

"What..." Leola couldn't finish her question, but she knew what it was.

Aidan looked to Leola, wonder in his eyes and a smile on his face.

He signed, "He says hello."

Chapter 7

Out Loud

Sera rushed forward to the dismay of her sister, but she couldn't believe her eyes. A dragon—an actual dragon sat in front of them now. She dropped to her knees next to Aidan, not caring about the rocks digging into her skin.

The creature's skin was covered in shiny, red scales; steam rose in tiny tendrils from its body. It was the size of a small horse, with crinkly wings in need of stretching and dangerous-looking claws on the ends of its four feet. Though it appeared newly born into the world, its fiery, orange gaze held wisdom and understanding, as if it knew all that she was and would be and was not surprised.

Aidan smiled at her before facing the dragon again. She, however, stared at her friend. There was something different about him. His eyes were bright, and the dragon tilted its head to the side, silently communicating with him. A soft chuckle left his mouth before he turned around to find his sister and Enya standing directly behind them, a mix of terror and joy on their faces.

"He says it's rude not to answer when someone says hello." Aidan signed to them.

Leola grimaced, "Hi?"

Enya lifted a hand and waved nervously.

Sera faced the dragon and whispered, "Hello. What's your name?"

The dragon stretched its wings and yawned, but Sera heard nothing. Whatever words were being spoken by the magical creature, it seemed that only Aidan heard them.

Her suspicions proved true when Aidan signed a translation for them.

"He says his name is not known because it has not been earned." Aidan paused, confusion on his face. "I have no idea what that means."

Sera laughed. "I don't either."

The excitement turned to worry when the sounds of more shouting filled the cave. Their parents would be looking for them after that earthquake, and what would they do when they found a dragon in their midst?

The four exchanged worried looks before Aidan and Sera jumped to their feet.

"We have to get out of the cave. They need to know we're okay," Enya reasoned. Leola nodded, and together, they turned to walk toward the entrance, Enya whispering something to her. Sera twisted her hands together, peeking over her shoulder again to look at the dragon.

Aidan lifted his hands to speak but paused and tilted his head, as if he were listening to someone behind him—listening to the dragon. Sera's heart pumped harder; she didn't want to leave the cave. Enya was right, though, and she didn't want her parents to worry.

"What is it?" She asked after tapping Aidan on the shoulder.

Leola and Enya quit murmuring to each other and faced Aidan and Sera.

"He says we can't leave. The cave entrance collapsed." Aidan's face paled slightly, and a heavy lump formed in Sera's stomach—no wonder the shouts of the others were muffled.

The only light in the cave came from the dragon itself, a soft reddish glow pulsing off its skin. Leola and Enya exchanged a look before turning back quickly to leave the cave, to see for themselves whether they were truly trapped.

Trapped! A terrible, tight feeling filled Sera's chest. She didn't want to be trapped, even if it meant being in here with a dragon. She grabbed Aidan's hand and pulled him toward the exit after their sisters. Heat pressed into them from behind, and she realized the dragon was following them. No, this wasn't good. Their parents would find him, or worse, other villagers would!

She tripped, trying to stop from running into the backs of Enya and Leola. Aidan pulled up on her hand, keeping her steady. She smiled tightly at him in thanks and felt chills settle into her bones. Where the entrance of the cave was supposed to be, nothing but rocks filled the space. Not even a tiny sliver of light escaped through.

They didn't tell their parents where they were going. Did Leola and Aidan?

"Enya, Mom and Dad won't know we're here!"

Enya chewed on her bottom lip. "Did you tell your parents where you were going?"

A look of shame passed over Leola's face, and Aidan dropped Sera's hand. Leola lifted her hands to sign, facing Aidan and Sera.

"No. We didn't tell them. I just said we had something we were working on." She startled for a moment, noticing the dragon standing behind Aidan and Sera.

Sera pushed past the others and started yelling. "HELP! SOMEONE! HELP!" A flapping sound, followed by a growl, filled the space.

"Sera, don't." Just as Enya spoke, more rocks and stalactites cracked and fell from the ceiling into the already insurmountable pile in front of them.

Sera stumbled backward, falling hard on her butt. She told herself to be brave, to be calm, but panic rushed through her body instead.

Enya and Leola grabbed her arms and pulled her backward away from the entrance and the falling rock, not giving Sera time to get her feet under her. The stones on the floor were going to leave bruises, she knew it.

Aidan waved his hands, drawing their attention.

"We can't get out that way. The dragon says he knows another way. We just have to trust him," he signed.

"Trust a dragon? That we just met?" Leola asked. Her voice went higher with each question. Her hands grew frantic.

"Yes. We need to follow him. We can't yell, or the cave will fall more." Aidan paused and turned toward the dragon.

The creature curled its tail around its body and sat staring at the four. Had it gotten bigger?

"Can we please just get out of here?" Sera begged.

"It's okay. Try to breathe." Enya rubbed her back to calm her sister's fears.

"I don't care how we do it. I really don't want to be in here any longer," Sera pleaded, her eyes locked onto Leola.

The voices outside grew more frantic. Either others were injured, or their parents realized they couldn't find them. Leola sucked her lips in, her demeanor tense. Finally, she sighed and turned away from the pile of rocks and debris.

"Okay, lead the way, brother."

Aidan moved toward the dragon; a silent conversation passed between them. The dragon stood and attempted to stretch its wings, but the cave hindered its efforts. It huffed in what Sera would describe as frustration before it ventured off into the depths of the cave back to where they had found it before.

When they reached the site of the demolished egg, Sera noticed a soft glow coming from the broken shards of shell or stone—whatever it was that dragon eggs were made of. Aidan approached the spot where the dragon stood waiting and placed a hand carefully on its neck, the other hand beckoning toward the others to join.

Sera didn't understand, but she trusted Aidan. Stepping up to the dragon, her fingers trembled as she stretched them toward the shiny, red neck. The scales felt warm and smooth beneath her fingertips. The ridges between the scales were not very defined. Maybe they grew rougher as the dragon aged? When the dragon didn't flinch, but instead stared deeply into Sera's eyes, she pressed her hand flat and took a deep breath.

None of them spoke as the other two joined Aidan and Sera, placing tentative hands on the dragon's neck and chest. Within moments, the air in the cavern grew hot. The soft red glow from the dragon grew into a blinding, bright white. Sera squeezed her eyes shut and clenched her teeth to hold in a scream.

The world around them splintered; the ground falling away from their feet instantly. Her belly twisted with nerves and something else—a force pulling her in every direction at once.

As quickly as the cave vanished around them, their feet met firm earth and soft grass yet again. The landing jolted their bodies, and all four fell to the ground in front of the dragon. Sera opened her eyes to find a cloud-covered sky above her head and dense forest all around them. They were in the cove.

All four looked around in wonder. Magic. The dragon's magic had brought them here.

Sera burst into laughter, relief rushing through her body like a river. It proved contagious, spreading to all four of them. When they had worn themselves out, a calm settled over the clearing. A strange peace and sense of contentment filled the space.

It was shattered by the sound of Sera's and Enya's names being screamed across the cove. Their mother had found them, and they hadn't had time to hide the dragon.

Chapter 8

Invisible

Aidan's heart dropped to his stomach. He saw Enya's and Sera's faces turn to horror, and shifted his gaze to the other side of the cove to discover what had caused their distress. Their mom, Mari, was running across the grassy space, tears streaking down her cheeks. Instinctively, he stepped in front of the dragon, desperate to hide him from the others. This was not going to be good.

He spun around to find orange eyes staring straight at him, unbothered by the chaos around them. The dragon had morphed into something larger now—the size of a large horse instead of a pony. He wasn't sure how that was possible, but he couldn't deny it.

I can't hide you! You have to run. Aidan directed his thoughts to the dragon. Sound pressed into his ears, making him cringe for a moment before he heard the voice loud and clear.

I'm not going anywhere. I am with you now, Firestar.

Dread coiled tighter in his stomach. They would take the dragon away. They wouldn't let him keep it. They might even condemn it to die. He wanted to touch the smooth scales again, to feel the warmth, and to tell the dragon to take him away from there. Far enough away that the creature would be safe.

It was too late. His friends' mom embraced them, her mouth moving quickly with words he couldn't hear. She lifted her eyes to Aidan and Leola and realized she wasn't speaking in a way he understood, shifting to the use of her hands.

"Are you two okay? We were all so worried when the earthquake happened." Her hands shook, but he understood her well enough.

He nodded and let Leola answer for them both.

"Yes, we're okay. We didn't mean to scare anybody." His sister paused; he imagined her mind spinning, trying to come up with an answer. "We were here in the cove, and it felt safer than going back through the trees when everything was moving so much already."

Mari nodded, "I'm just happy to find you all in one piece. Let's go before Veda and Milo lose their minds searching for you."

Aidan released a tight breath. He didn't consider how scared his own parents might be. Sera and Enya kept darting their eyes toward him and the dragon behind him. He stepped back and felt a soft nudge against his back.

Why are you afraid? The dragon's voice filled his ears.

Mari would scream any moment now.

But she didn't. Instead, she grabbed Sera's hand and tugged her along, walking toward the trail that led back home. Enya's eyes were wide with shock, and she stumbled before steadying herself to follow.

Leola clenched her jaw so tightly he imagined her teeth cracking from the pressure. She jerked her head, indicating they should follow, and then fell into line.

Why didn't Mari say anything? The only way to find any possible answers was to ask the dragon, but he was already too far back from the others. Wiping his sweaty palms on his pants, he peeked over his shoulder, but the dragon was gone. He searched the cove and the sky for any sign of the creature, but there was nothing, as if they'd imagined the entire thing.

He swallowed a lump in his throat and ran to catch up. Leola shot a confused look at him, and he took advantage of her attention.

"He's gone. I can't see the dragon at all," he signed.

Leola spun to face the cove and confirmed what he suspected. The dragon had vanished into thin air.

"Where do you think he went?" She asked.

"I don't know. But what if I never see him again?" Worry tugged at his chest, an annoying ache that filled him with dread. He wanted the dragon. There was a purpose behind all of this, and the dragon belonged to him. He couldn't explain this feeling to Leola. She would only laugh at him, or she would think that he was dumb. But the sensation was there nonetheless, pestering him.

Farther up the trail, he saw his mom and dad running toward them.

"Where in Endeilo have you been?" Their mother, Veda, gushed at them, her hands and mouth moving erratically.

"Next time, you have to tell us where you are going," Milo, their dad, chided.

"We're sorry," Leola murmured.

"It's okay. I'm just glad you're safe," Veda said. "Let's go home."

They said goodbye to Enya and Seraphina, with the promise of discussing the dragon soon written on all their faces. None of them dared to speak about it with their hands or mouths. Its sudden disappearance left a hole in Aidan's chest, but he said none of this to any of them.

Once they were back home, Aidan hurried into his room and quickly shut the door. Leola didn't bother him or try to intrude, though he could see that she wanted to. Their parents left to help search for anyone else who might be trapped in their homes, thanks to collapsing walls.

In the stillness of the room, he sat on his bed, trying to remember everything he had ever learned about dragons. Sera was the expert on all magical creatures, but she wasn't here. He jumped up and went to the small desk under his window. His scrolls and tablets were strewn all over the surface and on the floor; the chair lay on its side. Rifling through everything, he snatched up a tablet hidden beneath a couple of scrolls.

He sat on his bed and unrolled it on his lap. Skimming the pages, he hoped that maybe he had written something useful down. He found information about the history of dragons, their magical powers, and how they once flew in large numbers over all of Kida. Still, he couldn't find anything about the dragons' connections to humans.

Falling to his back, he closed his eyes, soaking in the feel of the blanket beneath his body. He needed to talk to Sera, but his parents forbade them from leaving the house until things settled down in the village. He wanted to find the dragon again, but how did you find a creature that can't be seen?

The bed vibrated, and Aidan's eyes snapped open. In the room, standing across from him, indifferent and unbothered, was the dragon. It was much too large to be in the tiny space. Its tail thumped against the door; its wings brushed against shelves and knocked more items to the floor. He flew to his feet, dropping the tablet to the ground.

Out of habit, he signed, "How did you get in here?"

The dragon tilted its head, curiosity filling its eyes.

You don't need to use your hands with me, Firestar. I do not understand them anyway.

Aidan clenched his fingers into fists. The phenomenon of hearing the dragon's rough voice in his ears left him feeling lightheaded. He relaxed his fingers and simply spoke his next words in his mind instead.

How is it possible for me to hear you? This was the moment. Now, he would get some answers.

You are my copania. I am bound to you and you to me. We do not need spoken words to communicate.

What was a *copania*? He'd never heard the word. Before he could ask another question, the dragon continued.

We were bound together in the stars before you were born. The god, Jadon, has appointed me to guide you on your journey. Something grave is coming for your world.

Aidan stepped back until the backs of his knees met the bed, and he lowered himself to sit.

What is coming? Why me? His heart pounded in his chest.

Why not you, Firestar?

Chapter 9

Storm

Seraphina and Enya huddled in bed together, reading through scrolls Enya had kept her schooling notes in from previous years. While Enya hadn't been as fascinated with dragons as Seraphina, she was a good student and wrote extensively about anything their instructors felt was important.

Dragons once ruled over the land, and they were the namesake of the kingdom of Kida. Magic belonged to them, not to people. When humans tried to create magic themselves, they corrupted the earth, and inky, dark magic seeped into the land. The dragons died one by one until only the remnants of the dragon stars remained to remind the humans of their former heritage.

"Why did people try to take magic for themselves?" Sera asked, feeling conflicted and a bit angry with their ancestors.

Enya shrugged, "People tend to take what isn't theirs. They steal lands, kingdoms, and peoples. Why wouldn't they try to steal magic, too?"

"I don't like that. Humans should just leave things alone. Dragons might still be all over the place if they'd just let them exist." Sera scowled and crossed her arms.

"I agree, but we can't change the past. The question is—why is there a dragon now? Why here? And why couldn't anyone but us see him?" Enya dropped her eyes back to the scroll.

"That was three questions, you know?" Sera sassed, and Enya rolled her eyes. "You forgot to add 'Why can Aidan hear this dragon but none of us can?'"

Enya's brow furrowed in thought. "It is really strange. There seems to be a connection between Aidan and the dragon. Nothing in my studies talks about any of this, though! Dragons have been thought to be extinct for decades. I'm not sure our teachers even know much about them."

Frustration coiled in both girls' chests. They wanted answers, but how do you find answers about creatures everyone believed were dead?

"Do you think we can sneak out to Leola and Aidan's house?" Sera whispered. Their parents were gone, helping others affected by the earthquake, but they had given strict orders for the girls to stay home, to stay safe.

"I don't know if that's a good idea." Enya stood up and walked to their window. The sky had grown dark and foreboding. Thunder rumbled in the distance. "It looks like a storm is brewing."

"I hate all of the storms here. Why are there always storms?" Sera whined.

"You know that's just the way it is here," Enya sighed. She squinted her eyes, a look of concentration on her face.

"Ugh, it doesn't mean I have to like it, though," Sera flopped backwards on the bed before realizing that Enya had gone strangely quiet. "What is it? What's wrong?"

She sat up and joined her sister at the window. The sky outside was dark, with swirling dark grey clouds covering the entire expanse. The treetops swayed in the wind, tiny sticks and pine needles falling to the ground. It reminded Sera of butter churning, and it looked angry.

Enya hurried out of their loft, climbing down the ladder and jogging to the front door.

"Mom and Dad should come home soon. There's something not right about this storm." Enya flung open the door and peered out. People ran down the streets while others pointed to the sky at the gathering storm clouds. She felt it, the strange shift in the air; a heaviness descended on their home.

Sera tugged on Enya's arm. "We need to go to Aidan's house. We need to figure out what happened to the dragon."

Enya stiffened at the suggestion. A part of her wanted to learn more about all of it, to understand the purpose of these events, but to leave when a storm was coming was asking for trouble.

"Sera, do you not see the sky?" She gestured wildly around them before stepping back inside and slamming the door.

"You feel it. I know you do. I feel it too. This is a different storm, and something tells me we need to find the dragon."

A flash of lightning filled the sky, followed by a loud crack of thunder. The storm was almost upon them. Enya grabbed their cloaks from next to the door and ran to the kitchen.

"What are you looking for!?" Sera screeched.

She didn't respond at first, searching through the top drawer of the cabinet in the corner. She yanked out a piece of paper, tearing a small corner off in the process, and found a pen and an ink jar as well. She scrawled a quick note to their parents and left it on the table under a small bowl before throwing her cloak on.

"Come on, let's go!"

Seraphina smiled, taking her cloak from Enya and following her out the door.

AIDAN CRINGED AS THE dragon knocked over the desk yet again. It seemed agitated by something. He righted the piece of furniture and tried to push the dragon toward the doorway to leave, but it spread its wings in protest, letting out what Aidan assumed was a roar based on the vibrations he felt in his hands.

Leola burst into his room—shock painted across her face. He tried to smile, but the dragon stumbled backward, knocking him to the ground. His sister wriggled past flapping wings and pulled him to his feet.

"How did the dragon get here!?" She signed.

"It just appeared. One moment, I was alone; the next moment, a dragon was standing in my room."

"Well, he's making a mess. We have to get him out." Leola flinched at something, while Aidan noticed the room had darkened suddenly. He moved toward the window, peeking out at the sky. Storm clouds gathered and churned above, making the day even darker than usual. The trees swayed in the forceful wind. He couldn't hear the thunder, but the lightning felt close. He sensed the tightness of the air, the way it hummed with power.

"When did this happen?" He signed to Leola.

"Now. It happened now. One moment, the sky was just pale gray clouds, the next, this storm blew in."

The dragon opened its mouth, and a tendril of smoke drifted out.

What are you doing? Why are you so upset? He screamed at the dragon in his mind. He felt the tension between them, and the air grew tighter in the room.

A dark power moved out there. The dragon didn't speak to him, but he could sense its distress. More smoke drifted from the nostrils of the creature.

We have to get you outside, or you'll burn our house down!

He grabbed Leola's hand and tugged her toward the door. He hoped the dragon would follow them out of the room. Leola took the lead and rushed toward the front of the house. When she opened the front door, rain lashed its way in, followed by a drenched Enya and Seraphina.

"What are you two doing here?" He asked.

"There's something strange about this storm," Enya responded. Her hands trembled slightly from the chill. She and Sera exchanged a look.

Sera nodded and turned her attention back to Aidan and Leola, opening her mouth to speak when something big, warm, and heavy slammed into Aidan's back, knocking him to his hands and knees. He scrambled to his feet before facing the dragon again.

The furniture in their small living space was crushed beneath the dragon's heavy frame. Its tail whipped back and forth, scraping the wall and narrowly avoiding Leola.

Seraphina stepped forward with her hands outstretched in a calming gesture as if she were speaking to a terrified pony instead of a fire-breathing dragon.

Aidan watched her lips move, reading the words she spoke to the beast.

"Shhhh... It's okay. You're safe. It's okay."

Enya and Leola each placed a hand on Sera's shoulders. Aidan wanted to tell Sera to get back, but he froze. The dragon folded its wings into its sides and stilled its restless feet. Its head tilted to the side, looking more curious than agitated now.

The storm raged outside as rain pelted the windows and roof.

Are you done destroying everything in our house now? Aidan asked the creature.

It huffed out a plume of scarlet smoke and eyed Aidan.

She will be useful to the League. We should bring her with us.

Chapter 10

The League

Sera watched the exchange between Aidan and the dragon. Though she couldn't hear his voice, she knew they understood each other in a way that she and the others couldn't quite comprehend. It was weird and magical at the same time. The only thing she wished was that she could hear the dragon, too.

She glanced around the front room of the house. The dragon had done a lot of damage, and she wasn't sure they would be able to convince her friends' parents that it was an accident. How did you explain all of this without telling them about the massive creature sitting in their home right now?

Enya and Leola whispered to each other, and Sera felt a bit like the outsider this time. Finally, Aidan turned to face them and signed.

"He says he wants to take us to meet some sort of dragon group?" Confusion filled her friend's eyes, followed by a thoughtful expression as he tilted his head back toward the dragon.

"What kind of dragon group?" Leola asked, her brow furrowed.

Enya shifted her weight from foot to foot next to Leola, concern filling her eyes. Her gaze darted around the room, and

Sera knew that they were thinking the same thing. This was a disaster.

"I'm sorry. He says it's not a dragon group. It's the League of Dragons," Aidan corrected.

"A League of Dragons? I've never heard anything about that before." Enya sounded unsure.

"Do other dragons still exist?" Leola added.

Aidan shrugged, "He says there is a League of Dragons. He didn't explain more than that."

The older friends asked more questions and discussed possible answers, but Sera fixated on the dragon's eyes. It watched her with curiosity, its gaze intense.

She tapped Aidan's arm to draw his attention before asking, "What else did he say? Why is he looking at me like that?" A tiny bubble of excitement grew in her chest and spilled over into her words.

Leola and Enya went silent at her outburst, but Aidan grimaced. The excitement bubble deflated a little.

"He said that we should bring you to the League. That you would be useful. I don't know what that means, though."

Sera's heart raced at the prospect of meeting other dragons, but the idea that she might be useful to them dampened her mood. A little of Enya's caution crept into her.

"Where is this League at?" She asked, one part hoping it was far away in some magical world, the other part terrified about where this journey might lead.

Aidan faced the dragon again, and the same thoughtful expression settled on his face. Before he could respond, Enya spoke up.

"She is not going anywhere. This is crazy!"

"I can go if I want to. Besides, I might be useful," Sera protested.

Enya opened her mouth to argue, but Leola intervened, "Enya's right, Sera. This sounds really strange, and we can't all leave to go to some league of dragons without our parents knowing. And you know as well as I do, there is no way they will let us go."

Sera's heart sank. Everything Leola said made sense, but she couldn't shake the feeling that she was supposed to go with the creature.

A loud crack of thunder boomed, and large balls of ice started pounding against the windows. A crash sounded when one of the windows shattered from the ice.

"This is the worst storm we've had!" Enya yelled, her hands stumbling over her words.

Aidan and Leola ran to close wooden shutters over the windows, careful to avoid stepping on the broken glass. The dragon stood up, its massive tail swinging behind it and knocking over another piece of furniture.

Sera hurried up to it, resting her hands against its warm side. Suddenly, Aidan jerked his head toward her and the dragon. His eyes widened in fear, and he stumbled toward them.

"Wait! Don't touch the dragon!" He signed wildly. Sera scrunched her eyebrows in confusion, trying to read his words.

Leola and Enya saw Aidan's dash toward the dragon and followed after him.

"What's wrong?" Sera asked, but she knew something had changed. The air around her crackled with magic, causing the hairs on her arms to stand on end.

Aidan collided with her, pressing her even harder into the dragon's side, and Leola and Enya reached forward—one of them grabbing Sera's arm, the other latching onto Aidan. In the blink of an eye, the room faded to black, and wind yanked hard against their legs.

Sera screamed, but she wasn't sure if any sound came out of her. Spinning fast and hard, she squeezed her eyes shut and prayed they were okay. The dragon was taking them somewhere. When the air around them stilled, she braved a peek out of one eye.

Her head felt woozy, and it took her a moment to feel steadier on her feet. When she pushed backward away from the dragon, her stomach dropped at the sight of the world around them.

Aidan coughed a few times and rubbed his eyes. When he opened them, he looked as amazed as Sera felt. They stood on the edge of a mountain, pine trees stretching out as far as the eye could see. The air was crisp, and perhaps most noticeably, the sky was crystal clear. Not a single cloud marred the sapphire expanse overhead.

The dragon snorted a plume of smoke, and Sera stopped staring at the sky and trees long enough to realize something very wrong had happened.

Leola and Enya were gone.

PANIC RACED THROUGH Sera, and she tugged hard on Aidan's arm.

"Where are Leola and Enya?" She signed frantically.

Aidan's eyes widened as he looked around, finally aware of their missing siblings. He turned his attention back to the dragon, and Sera hoped he was asking about the others. It was bad enough that they traveled without telling their parents they were leaving.

The dragon snorted and spread its wings outward, stretching them from tip to tip. The air here was crisp, and the dragon gave them a comforting warmth.

"He says they fell from the connection while we traveled. He doesn't know where they are," Aidan's hands shook.

"This is not good. Tell him to help us find them." She needed to think. Enya would know what to do in this situation, but Enya was gone.

Aidan shook his head. "He says there isn't time. We have to get to the meeting."

"Meeting!? What meeting?" Her hands flailed, and Aidan grabbed them, squeezing them. He gestured for her to slow down. She took a breath and tried again. "What meeting is he talking about? Who are we supposed to meet?"

The ground trembled beneath their feet, and a roar filled the air. Sera jumped and grabbed Aidan, tucking herself behind his back, the red dragon standing in front of them. The sound of wings flapping filled the air, and she poked Aidan in the back, then pointed to the sky.

A shadow descended over them, and a dragon three times their dragon's size landed heavily on the ground in front of them. Moments later, four other dragons joined it.

They were in the presence of what could only be the League of Dragons.

Chapter 11

Gathering

Aidan snatched Seraphina's hand, gripping it tightly and staring at the five dragons gathered before them. He wanted to be brave for her, but the sight of the beasts sent his heart stumbling and made his breath ragged. The small red dragon that had brought them here lowered itself toward the ground in what seemed to be a bow. He wasn't sure what they should do, but he figured following the lead of the smaller creature would be a good idea. He bowed low, dropping his eyes to the ground and pulling Sera down with him.

The first dragon that had arrived was taller than some of the pine trees surrounding them. Its scales were deep purple and glistened with what looked like diamonds in the sunlight. It snorted at their movements, and a plume of violet smoke drifted out of its nostrils. The other four dragons were only slightly smaller than this one, and for this reason, Aidan believed it to be the leader of their group.

Sera's breaths came quickly, one after another; panic grabbed hold of her. He squeezed her hand and straightened them both, trying desperately to calm her down. The purple dragon tilted its head, and then a strange vibration passed through the air—a barely felt hum coursing around them.

What's happening? He asked the red dragon, but it offered no response. It seemed to have forgotten that two humans were in their midst.

He wanted to speak to Seraphina, to ask her questions, but he was afraid to move his hands. He had never felt so limited as he did right now. Sera chanced a look in his direction, but she didn't try to speak to him either.

The other dragons stood tall and still as statues. They varied in colors from dark blue to indigo, and from green to orange. None of them paid any attention to the humans either. If it hadn't been for Sera standing next to him, he might have wondered if this was all a dream. It could still be one, he supposed. Who was to say that dreams couldn't feel real?

Another hum passed through the air, coming from the large purple dragon. A responding hum came from the red dragon. He must have missed it the first time, so caught up in the strange situation they found themselves in.

The dragons were talking to one another. Seraphina realized it at the same moment because her mouth opened in a gasp of excitement, and she smacked her other hand over her lips to mute the sound. The noise drew the attention of the dragons, particularly a green one off to the side.

It stood and stretched its great wings and opened its mouth into a lazy yawn. Then, it moved closer to them, one step at a time. Snow in the treetops fell in clumps with each pounding foot. The red dragon noticed the other and tilted its head in the direction of the children. Another strange hum passed through the air between the two dragons.

Cedar wants to know your names, Firestar.

Aidan jumped at the sudden intrusion in his head. He looked at the red dragon and then at the massive green one, standing so close he could feel its breath on his face. The dragons did have names! He wondered why they were allowed to know this one's name when the red dragon wouldn't share his.

Seraphina tapped his shoulder. "What happened? What did it say?"

"How did you know it said anything to me?" Aidan responded.

"I can tell on your face when you are listening to the red dragon. There's a look you get," she signed quickly.

He felt his face flush with embarrassment, though he wasn't sure why. He tried not to dwell on it, and instead, he answered her question.

"Apparently, the green dragon wants to know our names."

Her eyes widened, and she snapped her eyes back to the dragons standing around them. The green dragon eyed them before lowering its face level with theirs, breathing deeply. Was it... smelling them?

The red dragon waited for Aidan to respond; in fact, all of the dragons waited. Aidan froze at the sight, and he felt quite small in comparison to these great beasts. Seraphina nudged him in the ribs with her elbow, jolting him out of his reverie.

"My name is Aidan, and this is Seraphina," he signed.

The dragons looked at each other before turning their attention to the red dragon.

They cannot hear your thoughts like I can, Firestar, and they do not understand your hands.

He hadn't thought about how dragons communicated with humans in general.

Can they understand our spoken language? He asked silently this time. He felt Sera's curious gaze on him, but he didn't take his eyes off the smaller creature.

They understand the vibrations that pass through the air when your language is spoken. That is how I understand your friends.

Aidan felt frustrated. This dragon had heard the names he had spoken, but it was showing no interest in revealing the names to this gathering of its kind. Why couldn't the dragon just tell them their names?

Apparently, Sera couldn't wait for something more to happen and spoke up.

"I don't know if you understand our hand language. But he said that his name is Aidan, and my name is Seraphina." Her hands trembled slightly as she signed and spoke, but the green dragon raised its head back up and gave a quick nod in understanding.

The other dragons spoke amongst themselves again, the air quivering around them. When they finished, the dragons spread their wings and lifted themselves into the sky, sending cold blasts of air against the three left behind.

"What's happening? Why are they leaving? We need to find our sisters!" Sera shouted.

Come, Firestar. The clan has agreed to meet with you both in the Nest.

Aidan told Sera what the dragon said, and her face filled with anger. Instead of thinking about what he wanted to say, he signed so Sera could hear too.

"We need to find our sisters. Why didn't they end up here with us? We're not going anywhere without them."

Sera nodded her agreement before crossing her arms and staring hard at the dragon.

I don't know where they went, but we cannot find them without help from the League. We've been invited to the Nest, where we will stand before them to hear their decisions concerning you.

"Decisions on us?! What did we do?" Aidan asked.

"Wait, what decisions?" Sera interjected.

But the dragon offered no further insight. It stepped up closer to them, stretching its wings and waiting for them to do something. When neither of them moved, the dragon huffed and angled its head downward.

Aidan stretched his hand out until his fingertips brushed along the smooth red scales. The warmth drew him in until he pressed his hand flat against the dragon's chest. Seraphina stepped forward and did the same; a look of fierce determination blazed in her eyes.

Instantly, the world turned dark, and the strange pull of magic yanked hard on their bodies. Aidan worried he would lose his grip on the dragon, but some force held them both in place throughout the movement.

When the world stopped spinning, they found themselves standing in a large cavern filled with countless small openings that led into what looked like more caves. The air was damp and cool, reminding Aidan of the cave where they had found the egg.

What was more shocking than the cavern, the countless smaller caves, and the fact that they had arrived through a strange form of magic was the sheer number of dragons moving about the space. Small dragons, large dragons. They flew through the air. They walked along the ledges, and a constant hum of vibrations so loud that Aidan felt them deep in his bones, even more than when they had met the Dragon League among the trees before.

The sudden appearance of a small red dragon and two even smaller humans sent silence through the chamber within moments. Every strange eye turned in their direction, and true fear settled into both Seraphina and Aidan.

They were in the Dragon Nest, and every great beast with even sharper-looking teeth was aware of their presence.

Chapter 12

The Nest

Seraphina stared, open-mouthed, at the scene in front of them. Only a day ago, she didn't think any dragons existed, and now she stood amid hundreds of the creatures of varying sizes. The dragons stared back just as intrigued.

The red dragon led them toward the far side of the cavern, where a large archway opened into a dark tunnel. The air grew warmer as they walked closer to the entrance. She turned to Aidan to see his reaction. He looked as amazed as she did by the entire situation.

That look that Aidan always got when the dragon was speaking to him through their mind connection appeared again on his face. She waited impatiently, wanting to know exactly what the dragon said.

They still needed to find their sisters. Who knew where Enya and Leola ended up and whether or not they were okay? She wrestled with conflicting feelings of excitement and worry. What if something terrible had happened to them? She shook her head, attempting to dislodge the dreadful thoughts.

She startled when Aidan tapped her shoulder.

"The League of Dragons gathers here in the nest to discuss important matters in the world. Apparently, it's been a long time since humans were able to bond with dragons. The red dragon thinks this is important to see what the League believes should happen," he signed.

She scrunched her brow, her mind struggling to piece together the long stream of words. When she felt she understood, she nodded.

"What about Leola and Enya? Do they know where they are?" She asked, a little afraid of the answer.

Aidan bit his bottom lip, concern flitting across his eyes. "The red dragon said they will know what to do," he paused, glancing at the creature leading them under the archway. "But he didn't say they knew where they were."

Sera felt as if a rock had dropped into the bottom of her stomach. The dragons didn't appear concerned about their sisters, only curious about the strange connection between Aidan and the red dragon. They could decide that it wasn't worth the trouble to find the missing siblings. She took a deep breath, rolling her shoulders back, determined to gain their help no matter what.

The tunnel in front of them was dark as night. No light made itself known in the space. It smelled like fire, and it grew warmer the deeper they went, the path sloping downward with every step. She reached a hand out for the wall, stepping sideways a few times to get close enough. The stone beneath her fingers was soft as a babbling stream. It made her think that a wall didn't exist at all. The feeling left her dizzy, and she stumbled a step.

They couldn't talk to each other in the dark, but she reached her other hand out and listened for the sound of Aidan's footsteps. When her fingers brushed against his arm, he jumped, but she fumbled for his hand quickly and squeezed in reassurance. He squeezed back, and together they followed the tunnel into the belly of the earth.

It felt like they'd been in the darkness for ages, but she knew it couldn't have been that long. A soft light glowed ahead of them, and she had never felt so relieved to see the shadows on the walls as the light worked to pierce through the darkness.

The dragon slowly came into view as her eyes adjusted, followed by Aidan's face. She squinted as the light grew brighter and larger, taking up more space in the tunnel until they were shrouded in it and forced to close their eyes.

"What's happening?" She called out, realizing Aidan couldn't hear her, but neither of them could open their eyes to see, and the words had tumbled out instinctively.

They tripped on their feet, but the red dragon slowed and allowed them each to place a hand on its warm sides. He guided them through the light, and she noticed after a few more steps that the intensity of the light passing through her eyelids dimmed. She and Aidan peeked out cautiously, blinking several times until they could keep their eyes open comfortably.

The tunnel opened into a smaller cavern than the previous one, and in the center of it stood a large crystal bigger than the red dragon leading the way. It sparkled, but the light causing it to shine came from within the crystal itself. Sera felt the hair on her arms stand up, and she was reminded of the strange sensations she felt in the cave when they discovered the egg.

Surrounding the crystal, the same five dragons from before stood, most of them as still as statues. The only one showing any twitch of its muscles was the purple dragon. It was most definitely their leader, or at least, it was the creature in charge of this particular gathering. The eerie vibrations filled the cavern as the dragon spoke to the red one before examining the two humans with interest.

Sera couldn't wait another moment, and when she noticed a lull in the humming, she spoke up, signing as well for Aidan to understand her.

"We lost our sisters when we traveled here with the red dragon. Do you know where they are?" Her words tripped over each other, and she felt her face heat with embarrassment. She should have stayed silent.

The red dragon eyed her, then turned its gaze to Aidan.

"The purple dragon wants you to come forward, Sera," Aidan signed.

Her fingers trembled, and her heart raced at the idea of getting any closer to these humongous creatures than she already was. She swallowed the lump in her throat and shuffled forward, one timid step at a time. When she stood in front of the red dragon, she stopped, aware of all eyes on her.

The purple dragon hummed something and brought its great head closer to her, its purple eyes locking onto hers. She shuddered, but she didn't back down. She waited for some form of understanding to come over her, but it didn't. The humming was meaningless in her ears.

Aidan stepped up next to her, drawing the purple eyes away.

"The purple dragon wants to know their names," he signed.

"Can you hear the purple dragon like you hear the red one?" She asked, her curiosity getting the better of her.

"No, but the red dragon tells me what it says." Both of their gazes shot to the red one.

"Why don't..." but she was interrupted by a loud hum that forced her to cover her ears. The red dragon answered, and Aidan translated for her.

"It doesn't understand why we speak with our hands and not our mouths," he shrugged.

She faced the creature.

"My friend cannot hear. We speak with our hands so he can communicate. My sister's name is Enya, and his sister's name is Leola. We really need to find them. Please."

Aidan nodded his agreement, and the dragon gave a huff of annoyance before stepping back. The crystal's light pulsed three times before dimming. The red dragon moved to stand near Sera and nudged her toward the crystal. She hesitated, worry tightening her belly.

Then, Aidan grabbed her hand and pulled her forward. She resisted for only a moment before following. When they stood an arm's length away, Aidan lifted his hands to explain.

"They said we need to touch the crystal." Aidan's eyebrows scrunched together.

"Touch it? We're supposed to touch it? What's going to happen when we do?" Sera looked over her shoulder, hoping she could see a tunnel where they could make their escape. Suddenly, dragons felt a little more terrifying than she thought they would be.

Aidan lifted his hands as if to say what choice did they have. Sera swallowed audibly, and Aidan shook his hands out.

Then, both reached out and pressed their hands against the crystal's textured surface. It felt hot to the touch—not enough to burn, though. It reminded her of a hot cup of tea, warm and soothing.

Nothing happened at first, and she and Aidan exchanged a glance. She was about to ask what they were supposed to do when a strange tingling started in the palm of her hand. Aidan's eyes widened, and she knew he felt it too.

The prickling sensation worked its way up her arm and soon spread throughout her chest and back. The warmth she felt in the crystal transferred into her body. After a few moments, the feeling went away.

Both of them dropped their hands at the same time, like the crystal repelled them from itself. She examined her fingers, searching for any evidence left behind, but her skin looked the same as it always did.

"This will make communicating with you easier," a rumbly voice said.

It took a moment for them to realize who was speaking to them. Aidan turned his attention to the purple dragon. He looked thoughtful, and she knew he heard the voice in his head, though she was certain there was sound that passed through the air.

"We have much to discuss. Come. You may call me Lila," the purple dragon said before turning and walking farther away from the crystal.

The other dragons had moved back and now stood in a semicircle near the wall. The crystal cast them in just enough light for Aidan and Sera to see them.

"How is that possible? How can we understand you?" Sera asked, signing clumsily as she followed.

"Magic, small one. The crystal grants many things, but this is perhaps its most useful purpose for our situation," Lila answered.

Sera realized the dragon never opened its mouth, yet she heard its words. Perhaps the vibrations in the air were still occurring, but they were transformed into audible words for her and Aidan's benefit.

"Can we hear all of the dragons speak now?" Aidan asked, speaking aloud for the first time in a couple of years.

Sera started at his voice. When he had completely lost his hearing a year ago, he said he preferred to speak with only his hands because he said it felt strange to open your mouth and not hear the sound coming out anymore. She wasn't sure if it bothered him that he had lost his hearing, but he adapted.

Now, he spoke shakily for the first time, his voice sounding a little strained from disuse. Then, she remembered—the dragons couldn't understand their hands. While Aidan could hear the dragons in his head, they wouldn't understand him unless he spoke verbally or through Harkin.

The purple dragon tilted her head, a softness entering her eyes that wasn't there before. "Only those who are members of the League can communicate with you," she said.

When Sera, Aidan, the red dragon, and Lila completed the circle, a somber feeling settled among the others. As much as she wanted to celebrate this moment, it seemed that something serious troubled the creatures.

"Can you help us find our sisters?" She asked.

The dragons turned their attention to Lila, waiting for her to comment.

"Yes, I believe we can. But we gathered you here because something more important needs our attention, and we believe that you are vital to what comes next."

"We're not special or anything. What can we do?" Sera asked.

"The crystal called to you when you first walked past that cave, did it not?" Lila angled her head away from the ceiling, her wings twitching like she was eager to stretch them out once more.

"It wasn't a crystal, it was an egg," Sera reasoned.

"It was more than that. That was merely a pathway from the main crystal to your kingdom. We sent Harkin to wait for the next generation of dragon riders to emerge at the dawn of the tenth era."

None of this made any sense to Sera. The tenth era? She had never heard of that. Was Harkin the red dragon?

Speaking of the red dragon, he gave an irritated snort, and a puff of smoke drifted into the air.

Aidan smiled, "So that's your name then? Harkin." He only signed this time since Harkin could understand him without spoken words.

Sera swore the red dragon narrowed its eyes but refused to respond.

"Why do you need us?" Aidan asked Lila.

"Something is coming to your kingdom, and if it takes root, the balance in the world will shift toward destruction. Someone has opened the well of dark magic, and it is coming for all of us."

Chapter 13

A Quest

Aidan and Seraphina looked at each other before turning back to the dragons. A well of dark magic sounded bad, and who would want to bring darkness into the world anyway? Enough bad stuff happened on its own. Aidan wished Leola were here. He wished he could talk to her, have her by his side, and know that she was safe.

He exhaled hard before directing his next words to Sera silently, "We need to find our sisters before we worry about dark magic. They can help us."

Sera nodded next to him.

"Yes, the sooner we find them, the better," she agreed, signing back.

Lila looked hesitant, like she suspected they were going to ask her to do something she didn't want to do, or she didn't like being intentionally left out of the conversation. Either way, he figured that was probably understandable when you were a huge dragon, leading a large colony. He still wasn't sure what the League existed for, but it was important to them.

"If you help us find our sisters, all four of us will work to stop whatever this well of darkness is," he spoke, despite it feeling weird and strangely difficult.

Lila huffed in annoyance, and he thought she might have rolled her eyes, too. "Fine, you will need Harkin to assist you, and it won't be easy. Though compared to what you will need to accomplish later, it will seem effortless." Her voice felt strange, echoing around in his mind.

He felt lighter at the confirmation of the dragons' help. Harkin looked less than thrilled about the situation, but he remained silent.

"Okay, let's do this then," Seraphina declared.

"You will need to travel to the bog where the shadows never rest. When you arrive there, you must follow the blue lilies until you reach the meadow of peace. We are almost certain that they have fallen into the Enchantress's snare. She is tricky to escape from, and it will not be easy to retrieve your siblings. Harkin, you will fly them to the bog."

The great purple dragon turned her eyes to them both. "She will have her home warded to keep dragons from entering with magic, and she will require a riddle to be solved if she truly does have them trapped."

This Enchantress did not sound like anyone Aidan wanted to meet. Sera rocked side to side on her feet, looking just as nervous as Aidan felt. But they had to do this; they had to find their sisters.

"Okay," Aidan replied.

The large green dragon stepped forward, dropping its head to look them in the eyes. "It will be dangerous. It may not be worthwhile to save your hatch-mates."

Sera spoke up, "We'll do whatever we have to do to save them. No matter what."

The dragon stared silently for a moment before lifting its head away from them. "Very well. My name is Cedar. I will guide you to the map room."

A room of maps? Why did dragons need maps? How did they use maps when they didn't have hands? Aidan and Sera nodded nervously but remained frozen in place. They waited for the dragon to move, to lead them somewhere.

Instead, the dragon made a gurgling sound in its throat that might have been a laugh before speaking again. "You will need to touch my chest, small ones."

He lowered himself to the ground, making his chest more accessible to them. Aidan stepped forward first, and the closer he got, the more details he noticed in the dragon's scales. They sparkled with traces of gold amidst the emerald, and when he reached his hand out to touch the chest, the scales felt rougher, more jagged than Harkin's scales.

Seraphina joined him, pressing her hand onto the rough scales and taking a deep breath. Magic swirled around them, and they were plunged into the now familiar darkness with power pulling at them from all sides. When they arrived at the map room, a warm glow filled the room, coming from Cedar himself.

"I see why it's called the map room now that we're here," Sera signed.

"Yeah, this isn't what I expected," Aidan replied.

The wall was covered in maps, but none were on parchment, written with ink. They covered the walls, and as Aidan walked closer to the wall, he realized the map was made of burn marks on the stone. Fire created this map.

Their village, Ebonfore, was marked by a tiny triangle in the far-left corner of the map. He scanned the map searching for any name or sign that would show where the dragons' home was, but other than a few village names that he knew from their schooling and Natharia, the capital of the kingdom of Kida, he didn't recognize the other points on the map. They were written in symbols and lines, rather than letters.

"Where are we on this map?" Seraphina asked Cedar.

The dragon shifted his nose to the bottom right corner of the wall. "Dragon Mountain is here." His nose shifted to the center of the map. "This is where the bog is."

They stared at the jagged circle in the center of the map. Seraphina reached her hand forward and brushed her fingers across the mark. Then, she dragged her finger along some strange marks that Aidan hadn't noticed. He stepped closer and saw what she had—they were jagged, flowerlike shapes.

"These are the blue lilies, aren't they?" She asked the dragon.

He hummed in approval.

Aidan felt his stomach drop. The line of lilies stretched a long way before ending in a circle that must be the meadow of peace. It was not going to be a quick journey.

"We can't use magic to get there?" He asked.

"No, the area is guarded by a great power. You will fly with Harkin, then you must walk through the bog and lily path on foot. It's not an easy journey, small ones," Cedar declared.

Aidan shared a look with Sera, and the moment he saw her eyes, he knew she was scared but determined.

"Will Harkin remain with us along the way once we get there and have to walk?" He asked. He glanced at Harkin, but the red dragon remained quiet, waiting for Cedar's reply.

"Yes. I think that is for the best."

"But isn't he just a baby?" Sera blurted out.

Cedar made the strange rumbly sound in his throat again. "He is not a baby. He was simply asleep for fifty years, but he won't grow any larger than his current size. There are many different types of dragons, just as there are many different types of people. Do not underestimate his strength because he is small."

Sera cast her eyes to the ground, chastened. "I'm sorry, I didn't mean to offend."

Aidan touched her shoulder, and she lifted her chin. Cedar had lowered his head until he was eye to eye with her. The dragon didn't seem offended; he appeared thoughtful.

"You are stronger than you think you are, small one."

Aidan smiled, and Sera seemed lighter at the statement.

"Okay, we're ready," Aidan signed.

Cedar raised his head and looked at Harkin. The red dragon spread his wings and walked to Aidan's side. He knelt, pulling one wing back slightly to give them room to climb up. Aidan went first, and Sera squeezed in behind him, wrapping her arms around his waist. When they were somewhat secure, Harkin stood and spread his wings.

Fear made Aidan's stomach flip. He didn't know what to do with his hands. Harkin's smooth scales didn't offer much to hold onto.

It's okay, Firestar. Squeeze with your knees, and my magic will keep you secure.

He blew out a breath and relaxed, deciding he had no choice but to trust they wouldn't fall.

"We will use magic to leave the caves, and then we will fly, Firestar," Harkin called aloud.

Sera gasped, hearing Harkin's voice for the first time, and Aidan's smile grew wider. The world went dark, and they clung tightly to the dragon with their legs as the magic pulled at them.

It lasted only a moment before they were outside in the daylight, soaring high above the trees and mountains. Aidan felt Sera's chest vibrate with laughter, and he knew she felt as amazed as he was in this moment.

They were riding a dragon.

Harkin turned toward the west, where the sun was making its descent from the highest point in the sky. Hopefully, they reached the bog before dark. Aidan didn't want to know what might live in that shadowy place.

Chapter 14

The Bog

The world felt tiny and enormous at the same time. Seraphina watched in wonder as the trees shrank on the ground beneath them while the land stretched endlessly ahead. The air was cold this high up, but at least Harkin was warm beneath her, and she had Aidan close to help keep the chill away.

She kept searching for a barren area ahead of them, but as far as she could see, nothing but dense, lush forest covered the land. They flew for what felt like hours, and her butt was going numb. She was about to ask Harkin how much farther they had to go when Aidan pointed ahead. The movement threw her off balance, and she clutched him tighter with her arms and squeezed her legs around Harkin's warm body to keep from falling to the side.

Aidan looked over his shoulder at Sera, an apologetic smile on his face as he shrugged. When she felt secure enough, she lifted her chin over his shoulder to see what had caught his eye.

Up ahead, a strange patch of earth became visible. The ground was empty and looked soggy, with no trees or large shrubs visible. She had never been so excited to see such a lifeless place as she was in this moment. Apparently, riding dragons was not as pleasant an experience as she had believed it to be. It was amazing but exhausting, and she was ready to get her feet on solid ground.

Harkin swooped down to the land, letting the wind catch his wings and carry him gracefully to the earth. She slid off first and squealed, whirling her arms in circles to regain her balance. The ground squished under her feet, moving on its own as if a force disturbed it from underneath. Aidan landed with a squish next to her, and the ground roiled again at the contact.

They both struggled to regain their footing, and Harkin had to place a wing behind them to keep them from falling over.

"We have to walk on this the entire way?" Sera asked.

Aidan lifted one foot and then another, getting a feel for the surface beneath their feet.

"I guess so," he signed. He looked up at the sky toward the west and pointed. The sun was halfway down to the horizon. It had taken them far too long to arrive here, and with the messy state of the ground beneath their feet, they knew it would be slow going.

"I guess we'd better search for blue lilies," Sera said.

Aidan nodded.

"This way, Firestar." Harkin pointed with his nose and walked toward the far end of the bog.

At least they had a dragon to lead the way, thought Sera.

There was no path through the bog. Everything looked the same, with some areas moving on their own from something living underneath the patches of grass and weeds. Every step was a challenge, and the only thing keeping Sera from crying was knowing she would find Enya and Leola at the end of this journey.

Her feet were getting wet, as were Aidan's, and the temperature dropped with each passing hour as the sun crept closer to the horizon.

She tapped Aidan's arm. "What if we have to sleep in the bog tonight? How will we stay warm?"

Aidan looked worried, scanning their surroundings.

"I guess we can sleep close to Harkin? Or maybe he can light a fire?" He replied.

"No fires. The bog is too wet, and we don't want to draw attention to ourselves. You are both easy targets as it is," Harkin chimed in.

Aidan and Sera looked at each other.

"Easy targets for what?" asked Sera.

"For the *crason*, of course," Harkin answered. The dragon swung its head around, observing, listening.

"What's a *crason*?" Aidan asked, his brow furrowing as he tried to figure out how to spell out the word.

"It is a creature that lives in the bog. It slips under the grassy areas and snatches its prey, dragging them into the water below."

Aidan and Sera stared in horror at each other. From that moment on, every little sound made Sera jump. She wanted to run, but the ground would only snatch at her feet. Aidan flinched when Sera did, unable to hear the sounds she heard but becoming more on edge with every passing moment.

The sun was level with the horizon when the bog began to give way to firmer soil. Sera glanced back only once and saw a ripple pass under the soggy surface of the land. She shivered and quickened her pace to catch back up to Harkin and Aidan.

"We'll stop here for the night," Harkin announced.

"There are the blue lilies we were supposed to find!" Sera shouted. In her excitement, she forgot to draw Aidan's attention first, but Harkin answered her regardless.

"Yes, that's the path we will take. But we can't travel on it at night. It isn't safe."

"Nothing is safe about this journey," she sighed.

Aidan smiled when he saw her respond. "At least we found the path," he signed.

Sera shrugged and nodded. Harkin moved to the side farthest away from the bog and nearest the blue lily path. The lilies were magical, a soft blue glow emanating from their sapphire petals. They went on as far as Sera could see, bordering what must be a dirt path through the land.

She was hungry and thirsty, but they had come completely unprepared. Harkin lay down on the ground, his red scales turning slightly purple with the lilies' blue light painting him.

Aidan took Sera's hand and led her to the dragon's side. Harkin looked up, stretched out one of his wings, and the two sat down on the ground, leaning against the warm shoulder of the beast. His wing came down over them like a blanket, and he lowered his head to the ground, curling his neck in front of them.

Despite their hunger and the general uncomfortable nature of the ground, they both fell asleep quickly. Sera's last thought was that she hoped their sisters were faring okay wherever they were, and maybe they would find them tomorrow when the sun woke back up.

Chapter 15

The Enchantress

Dawn crept over the horizon, bathing the bog in golden light. Aidan felt chilly air brush over his skin as Harkin lifted his wing, removing his warmth from them. He opened his eyes and noticed Seraphina stirring next to him as well. She yawned and blinked her eyes a few times.

"We made it through the night at least," he signed.

She rubbed her face and focused again on the bog. He didn't think it looked as scary as it did last night, not with the sun coming across the grass in streaks.

Harkin stood up without waiting for them to stand, jostling them both to the side.

"We need to get moving, Firestar," he huffed.

Aidan helped Seraphina to her feet. "Can you give us a moment, please?" He was certain that she would need to relieve herself as much as he did at this point.

Sera cringed, looking awkward and shy all of a sudden. "I'll go over there." She pointed to the right side of the trail. He nodded and went to the left.

"Humans are so weak," Harkin grumbled.

When they rejoined the dragon, Harkin stretched his wings a couple of times before tucking them in tightly to his sides.

He walked to the blue lily trail without another word, leaving Aidan and Sera to jog to catch up. Aidan's stomach felt hollow. They hadn't eaten anything since yesterday, when they were home, and his parched mouth reminded him of how thirsty he was. They needed to find something to drink and eat soon. Sera rubbed her stomach next to him, and he knew she was as hungry as he was.

"Keep an eye out on the trail for food. Maybe there are berries we can eat?" He told her. She nodded with a grimace.

"There is no food on the trail. Nothing is safe to eat along this path. That is why we must finish this quickly. You small humans won't last long out here." Harkin spoke, and the words made Aidan despair.

He was hungry, and he wasn't sure how they would be able to think straight to solve a riddle if the Enchantress did have Leola and Enya. There was nothing they could do except follow.

The path was packed down and smooth as if it were well-traveled, though he couldn't see why anyone would want to walk to such a dangerous place. The blue lilies continued to glow softly even as the sun rose in the sky. Magic made the air feel thick and strange the farther they went. It reminded him of when the magic pulled at them, and they traveled quickly through darkness with the power of the dragons. Here it was everywhere, pressing down on them from above, making their feet feel heavy below.

Sera winced every few steps, and when he glanced at her shoes, he noticed how worn down they appeared. Something was wrong with this place.

The sun was halfway to the highest point in the sky when the path opened into a large field, and thousands of blue lilies spread over the grass like a blanket. The path narrowed, and Harkin slowed his steps. As they stepped into the meadow, the dragon seemed to go on high alert, lifting his head higher and scanning back and forth across the field.

Then, as if someone had erased it from the earth, the path vanished. Only grass and flowers spread out around them. Aidan and Sera turned around, both feeling relief to find the dirt path leading back the way they had come, but there was no guidance on how they should proceed. The trail didn't exist beyond this point.

"What do we do now?" Sera asked, fear filling her eyes.

"Be quiet," Harkin warned. His tone was firm and cautious.

Aidan's heart thudded in his chest, and he spun around searching for any sign of the Enchantress or their sisters.

What's wrong, Harkin? Where are they? Aidan asked in his mind.

She is watching, Firestar. Be alert. Don't let her trick you into thinking you are safe. The dragon's thoughts filled his mind. He eyed Sera to see if she was hearing the creature too, but her eyes darted back and forth from Harkin to Aidan in confusion.

"He says the Enchantress is watching us. That she will try to trick us. We need to be quiet," he explained.

Sera nodded, moving her hands carefully in response. "Okay, will she offer us a riddle?"

"Let me ask Harkin," Aidan said. *How will we know what to say in response to her riddle?*

Anything you speak now, she will count as your answer. You cannot speak unless you know the answer to the riddle. So, wait until she arrives. She is hoping you will make the same mistake as your sisters.

"But how do we know she has them if we don't ask?" He questioned.

She has them. I can smell them here.

He searched desperately for any sign of them. Sera tapped him on the shoulder, not understanding what he was doing.

"What's going on?" She signed, keeping her mouth silent.

"He says he can smell Leola and Enya."

Her eyes widened, and she joined him in his search. They surveyed all around when something caught Sera's eye, and she stopped, grabbing Aidan's hand and pointing. In the distance, a strange figure moved through the blue lilies and tall grass straight toward them.

Chills ran up Aidan's arms at the sight of the person, if he or she could be called that. They wore a long blue cloak with the hood pulled up, hiding their face. This had to be the Enchantress. Harkin faced whoever walked toward them, and Aidan and Sera stepped back until their backs pressed into the comforting warmth of the creature's chest.

Within moments, the figure stood before them, staring down from a great height. It was definitely the Enchantress. Power pulsed from her in waves. She stood taller than Harkin himself, and magic seemed to reach out toward them from her entire being. Light brown hands reached up and pulled the hood back, revealing light brown hair with silver streaks cascading down her back almost to the ground. She stared at them with gray eyes, and Aidan had never felt so insignificant in his entire life.

"What are young ones like yourselves doing out here all alone?" Her voice was airy, like she intentionally breathed out harder than normal on each word, and Aidan felt the words in his head more than heard them with his ears. It was similar to how he heard Harkin, but nowhere near as enjoyable to experience. Her voice was an invasion.

Do not answer her, Firestar. She uses magic to communicate with all living things, so there is no language that she does not know.

Aidan felt a drop of sweat bead on his forehead, and he grabbed Sera's hand, squeezing a reminder. He saw her throat bob out of the corner of his eye. The Enchantress narrowed her eyes at them before turning her gaze to Harkin, assessing him the way the women assessed the goats in the market meant for their families' dinners.

Harkin growled deep in his throat.

"I see that you are shy children. Probably kept hidden away by your families, far from me. I mean you no harm, but this dragon might be far too dangerous to be around. Where are your parents? Is the dragon holding you captive?" She feigned concern, brow furrowing and her frown deepening.

Her eyes never left Harkin while she spoke, and every word out of her mouth made Aidan feel dizzier. She was enchanting them even as she spoke. They had to do something.

In his mind, he pushed his thoughts toward Harkin. *How do we figure out the riddle? She's doing something to us even now!*

Harkin spread his wings and snorted a plume of smoke in warning to the Enchantress. Sera's palm was growing sweaty in Aidan's hand. At least, he thought it was hers; it may very well be his hand growing damp.

"My name is Willow. I am the keeper of lost things. I do not release them without proper payment."

Her eyes slid to Sera, and a tremor vibrated along their joined hands. For the first time in a while, the silence stretched, making Aidan nervous. This was taking too long. He could feel Harkin's presence in his mind, reminding him to remain quiet, but it was growing even more difficult to wait.

He could feel Sera's resolve to remain quiet fading quickly in how she fidgeted next to him when Willow's breathy voice entered his mind again.

"I see you have been warned about speaking when you shouldn't. Very well." Annoyance tinged her words. "I will offer you one riddle, and you may take your sisters with you."

A flash of light made Aidan and Sera cover their eyes, and when it cleared, they blinked several times, clearing their vision to find Enya and Leola standing beside the Enchantress.

Chapter 16

Rescue

D read coiled in Enya's stomach at the sight of Aidan and Seraphina. Part of her wanted to be happy to be reunited with them, but the more logical part knew this was a disaster. This wicked Enchantress was tricky and conniving. The moment she and Leola had landed in the meadow instead of wherever Aidan and Sera had gone, the Enchantress was there, waiting for them. She had suspicions that it was *she* who had pulled them from their siblings.

Leola, body tense next to Enya, practically shivered with nerves. They wanted to run to their siblings and the red dragon, but the magic's grip on them tightened at the slightest hint of movement.

Sera's eyes widened when she first saw Leola and Enya appear, and Enya hadn't missed how Aidan's hand tugged backward on Sera's, keeping her sister from bolting across the distance. She was thankful for that at least.

"The magic has rules. One riddle. One chance to answer. Answer correctly, and you are free—all of you. Answer incorrectly, and you will remain with me in the meadow."

Enya trembled with fear. The Enchantress kept her and Leola locked up in a hole in the ground, with nothing but each other to stay warm. It had been cold and damp. Both girls had cried until their eyes felt dry and puffy.

Sera and Aidan exchanged a glance, and the red dragon exhaled hard, blowing smoke into the air. She wondered how Aidan was understanding the Enchantress, but it must have to do with her magic because he didn't seem confused at all. They had obviously been warned before arriving, and neither of them spoke or signed to communicate at all.

"What has lived for ages, but is only two months old?"

Leola glanced at Enya, horror filling her eyes. What sort of riddle was this? How would their younger siblings solve it?

They were never going to make it home again.

While Aidan and Seraphina stared at each other and then at the dragon, Enya's mind scrambled to come up with an answer. She looked at Leola, but neither of them spoke. She knew her friend would be trying to solve the riddle as well.

What has lived for ages, but is only two months old? Could something be both old and young at the same time? It was impossible. Nothing could exist that way. It was a contradiction.

A smirk was forming on Willow's lips; she had them tangled in confusion, and she knew it. Despair formed a tight knot in the pit of her stomach. Leola knew it, too. Her friend's breathing increased, and fresh tears welled up in her eyes. Enya looked away, not wanting to cry any more than they already had. Then, a horrible thought raised its head. What would their parents think? They must be terrified and upset, losing their children on the same day. Would they stop looking for them eventually, or would it haunt them for the rest of their lives?

She squeezed her eyes shut, trying to shake the thoughts from her head.

"You're running out of time, children," the Enchantress taunted in a gleeful voice. "Do hurry up. Oh, and remember the dragon mustn't speak for you."

Of course, the dragon couldn't help them, Enya thought. He would surely know more than Aidan and Seraphina. She took a deep breath when she saw Aidan and Sera nod to each other before Sera stepped forward to give their answer. They must have signed discreetly between the two of them to come up with an answer.

Sera peeked back at the dragon and Aidan one last time, and Enya felt sick to her stomach. One chance. They only had one chance.

"Do you have your answer, child?" The breathy way in which the Enchantress spoke grated on her ears.

"I have our answer," said Sera.

"Go on. Tell us."

"What has lived for ages but is only two months old? Well, the moons have existed for a really long time, ages, I mean. But they change in appearance over two months. So, we say the answer is the moons. The moons are the answer. To your riddle." Sera's hands shook as she signed and spoke.

Leola sucked in a breath, and Enya's mouth dropped open. The answer was brilliant. It had to be right.

Shock turned to anger on the Enchantress's face. She opened and closed her mouth, not once, but twice, sputtering to find a response. The magic, however, did not need her permission to release, apparently. Suddenly, a weight lifted from all their shoulders, and the air felt less heavy and tiresome.

Enya laughed, covering her mouth with both hands, and Leola's broad smile told her she noticed the change as well.

"That's... that's..." Willow stammered, then seemed to give up. "That's correct. But how?!"

They didn't wait. Enya and Leola raced across the space until they collided with their siblings in bone-crushing hugs. They were free!

"I was so afraid!" Sera cried happy tears, and Enya squeezed her even harder if that was possible.

Leola and Aidan were signing so quickly back and forth in silence that she had no way of understanding anything they were saying.

"This is impossible! How could you two know that answer?!" Rage pulsed off the Enchantress, but when she tried to step forward, the magic held her back. She screamed, and all four children flinched, backing up toward the red dragon, which now spread its wings and roared.

"We have to get out of here," Sera exclaimed.

The red dragon turned to face the path Enya hadn't seen before. It lowered itself to the ground, and Sera and Aidan clambered up its side onto its scaly back.

"Hurry!" Sera yelled.

Enya and Leola followed, marveling at the strange smoothness of the dragon's scales and the warmth emanating from its body. It was a tight squeeze with all four of them on its back. The older girls had to kneel, keeping their feet tucked up and off the dragon's wings. They held on tightly to each other as it stood and ran down the path with blue lilies glowing strangely on either side.

Chapter 17

Escape

They were going to die. Leola was certain about this. She and Enya had been trapped for a day, and it felt like years had passed while they were stuck inside that filthy hole in the ground. Now, they were going to plummet to their deaths off the back of this dragon when they finally had a chance at freedom. The jostling movement of the dragon threatened to throw her straight off its back. If she wasn't clutching Enya so tightly in front of her, she was certain she would have slid right off its tail by now.

"Please let us make it. Please let us make it," she murmured over and over again.

Her heart pounded in her chest, and she wanted to look over her shoulder for the Enchantress, but she was too afraid to move. Instead, she kept all of her focus on locking her arms tightly around Enya's middle and squeezing the dragon's sides with her knees. Thank goodness, the dragon didn't have sharp scales, or this entire experience would be even more unpleasant.

The path of lilies suddenly turned into mushy grass, and she felt the dragon's feet falter when it hit the marshy ground. A scream reached them, so piercing that she was tempted to let go of Enya and cover her ears. She cringed against the pain that pulsed through her head as a result, and she knew if she looked behind her, she'd find that wicked woman chasing them.

A claw of magic snatched at them, and she felt the roar of the dragon as much as she heard it. But the red dragon didn't stop. It plowed into the bog, its talons digging into the spongy ground. Another whoosh of magic swept past Leola's head this time, a slight stinging sensation on her right ear. She and Enya both screamed.

"Come back here! You cheated! It's not possible that you solved the riddle!" Willow bellowed.

Leola had no idea how her brother and Seraphina had solved that riddle, but they had, and the magic had recognized their success. It didn't prevent the Enchantress from storming after them in a tantrum of magic and mayhem. Why couldn't the dragon fly them out of here?

The bog went on for as far as she could see when she peeked over her friends' shoulders. Another swipe of magic singed her back, and a cry escaped her throat. Willow was getting closer, and the dragon was getting warmer beneath her knees.

The smell of sweat filled her nose, and her stomach argued at the intrusion. She and Enya hadn't eaten since the day before. She wondered if Sera and Aidan had found any food. They were fueled by terror at the moment.

When she thought that the Enchantress's magic would reach them on the next swipe, a splash sounded behind them, followed by a muffled yell. Something big shifted the already unsteady ground beneath them. More splashing and screaming reached them, and she could feel magic heavy in the air once again. She couldn't take it any longer. She turned her head, squeezing tighter to Enya, and gasped when she saw the Enchantress and some bizarre creature tangled together in battle.

The monster opened its mouth to roar, displaying rows of jagged teeth throughout its long, narrow snout. Its body writhed around the Enchantress like a giant snake, except this monster had several legs, claws, and made the dragon they rode seem tiny. Leola shuddered at the sight, thankful the Enchantress was the object of its attention and not them.

Enya's hand smacked Leola's arms, and she realized that she was crushing her friend. She loosened her grip and focused forward again, hoping they would finally make it free from this dark place.

A little while later, the dragon slowed, its breath coming in sharp puffs of smoke. The sounds of the Enchantress and the monster faded until only the sounds of the kids' ragged breaths filled her ears. They had made it. They escaped the Enchantress.

The bog's ground turned firm, and the dragon slowed to a halt, lowering itself without warning. The air around them was lighter, and when they landed on the ground, all four of them sank to their butts.

"Is everyone okay?" Enya asked. Her hands shook with each word.

Sera and Aidan nodded, and Leola wasn't sure, but she thought she might have moved her head as well. Sweat made their clothes stick to them, and now that the immediate danger to their lives was passed, they realized how thirsty and hungry they were.

"Are you okay, Harkin?" Sera asked.

Who was Harkin?

Leola looked around, but she realized Harkin must be the dragon's name. A strange humming sound passed around them, coming from the creature's throat. Her mouth dropped open in shock.

"Are you talking to the dragon?" She asked, and Enya's head snapped up to look at her sister.

"Yes, the dragon speaks. When we were at the dragon mountain, they had us touch a crystal that allowed us to understand what they were saying," Aidan signed. "I can hear Harkin when he wants to talk to my mind, but for some reason, that's just me."

He shrugged, casting his eyes to the red beast before turning them back to his sister.

"Well, that's...interesting," Leola answered.

"I'm so hungry," Enya sighed.

"What happened to you two when you were with the Enchantress?" Sera asked, her voice sounding small.

Leola and Enya locked eyes, a slew of unspoken words passing between the friends.

"She kept us in a hole in the ground. It was cold and damp. I... I think she would have kept us there forever." Enya's eyes filled with tears at the memory.

"When we got separated, we landed in the meadow, and the Enchantress was there waiting. It was like she knew that we were coming," Leola explained.

"Or she pulled us away from you in the first place. It seemed planned," Enya added.

Leola nodded in agreement. Aidan and Sera remained silent.

"What about you? Where did you two end up?" Leola finally asked.

"Harkin took us to meet the League of Dragons. They met us in some forest first, but then they let Harkin bring us to a huge cavern filled with more dragons than we've ever seen. The dragons told us how to find you," Aidan said.

"This is bizarre." Leola rubbed her temples with her fingers, massaging a headache away that had formed. It didn't help much.

The dragon, Harkin, stood up and spread its wings. It looked at Aidan, and it gave Leola goosebumps to realize her brother was communicating with the creature silently in his mind.

"He says we can use magic now to get back to the League," Aidan said.

"Wait, the League? What about going home? Our parents are going to be terrified!" Enya protested. She had a point, but Leola was also curious about the dragons' home.

The same humming sound filled the air more forcefully this time. "He says we must return to the League first; then he will take us home," Sera translated.

She looked apologetically at Leola and Enya, but they couldn't blame her. The dragon didn't care what they thought, apparently. She only had one question that she couldn't wait to find the answer to.

"How did you solve the riddle?"

The other three turned their heads to Leola.

"That riddle was tricky. How did you figure it out?" Leola asked again.

The moment the words left her mouth, it came to her. The dragon.

Harkin snorted and flapped his wings a couple of times as if to confirm her suspicions. Enya realized it at the same time as herself. The Enchantress had stressed that the dragon was not to help them, but she couldn't hear him speak to Aidan's mind.

"It was the dragon. Harkin? He spoke into Aidan's mind to help," Enya whispered breathily.

Aidan and Sera grinned. "Yes, Harkin told Aidan, and Aidan only signed moons for me to see. I spoke for us then. We couldn't have done it without him."

Him. The dragon.

This all felt impossible, but here they were in the middle of nowhere with a red dragon that spoke to her brother's mind.

The dragon hummed again, and Sera reached her hand toward Enya. "Here, we need to have our hands on his chest. The magic will take us to the cavern right away."

Sera, Aidan, and Enya had already walked over, placing hands on the soft scales of the dragon's chest. She stood up, dusting off her pants before moving to join them. She hoped that wherever this dragon league was, there was food and water, too.

Her palm slid over the warm scales, and she opened her mouth to ask another question when the world went dark, and magic yanked hard at her body.

Chapter 18

Safe

They landed hard on a stone floor, cool air swirling around them as they stumbled backward from Harkin. Aidan lost his balance entirely and fell straight to his butt on the ground with a grunt. Seraphina offered her hand, and he took it, dusting himself off with his free one. Leola and Enya appeared unharmed, and most importantly, all four of them were together. He didn't care what happened to the Enchantress; he only wanted them out of harm's way. Or mostly out of its way, he supposed. He wasn't sure they were entirely safe, surrounded by dragons, but it was better here than in the bog and meadow.

I must rest, Firestar. I am too weak to take you home. Harkin's voice sounded strange in Aidan's head. It wasn't strong and loud like usual, but soft and weary.

Okay. Get some rest. I'll tell the others. Aidan wasn't sure why Harkin hadn't spoken aloud; Sera would have understood the dragon's language. He worried the creature was dangerously weak.

Harkin plodded away, his wings drooping and his tail dragging along the ground. Seraphina noticed the dragon's demeanor and tapped Aidan on the shoulder. "Is he okay?"

"I hope so. He said he's too weak to take us home," answered Aidan.

Leola and Enya joined them; every single one of them looked and felt terrible. Cedar, the large green dragon, appeared behind them.

"You achieved your goal!" He exclaimed, startling Leola and Enya with his sudden appearance and vibrating voice.

"What did it say?" Leola squeaked.

Aidan had forgotten they couldn't understand the dragons. "This is Cedar. He noticed that we found you both."

"Come, small ones. Your siblings must touch the crystal. Then you will be fed!" Cedar huffed and turned away, walking toward a narrow tunnel.

Sera and Aidan followed immediately, but their sisters hesitated.

"Come on, it's okay. They want you to see the crystal." Sera waved them forward with her hand before continuing after Cedar.

Enya and Leola searched the cavern, their eyes wide as they noticed the sheer number of dragons occupying the space. Then, they hurried after Aidan and Sera.

The tunnel Cedar led them to was the same as before, and soon they were plunged into darkness, but this time, they didn't have Harkin to guide them through the heavy blanket of black that filled the space. Instead, they held hands, forming a chain to keep together.

Their stumbling drew Cedar's attention, and the dragon began to glow a warm greenish light from his scaly body. It was still dark, but they could see more of the uneven ground than before thanks to the light coming from the dragon.

The end of the tunnel lit up with a bright light, and Aidan knew the crystal was close. They spilled out of the tunnel, tripping over a few misplaced rocks and into the chamber housing the crystal. No other dragons waited for them around the crystal this time.

Cedar paused in front of the giant crystal, and Aidan knew what the dragon wanted Leola and Enya to do. They stood nervously to the side, eyes darting between the crystal and the dragon. Aidan reached out and tapped Leola on her shoulder, pulling her attention to him.

"He needs you to touch the crystal," Aidan signed.

"What happens if I touch the crystal?" She answered, her eyes filled with nerves.

"It's okay," Sera said. "When you touch the crystal, they'll use magic to allow you to hear and understand their words. Those strange vibrations you feel in the air when they speak? You'll know what they mean."

Enya remained silent, never taking her eyes off the great green dragon. Leola glanced once more at it before responding to Sera and Aidan's explanation.

"Okay, will we be allowed to leave afterwards?"

Aidan looked at Sera before turning to Cedar.

"We will allow you to eat before we send you home. Harkin must rest a little longer and visit the healers before he can take you," Cedar answered.

Aidan signed to allow Leola and Enya to understand the rumblings coming from the creature.

Enya still didn't speak, but she stepped forward, stretched her hand out, and placed it against the crystal's rough surface. She opened her mouth in a gasp, but she stayed where she was. Leola followed, and Aidan knew exactly what they were feeling when they touched the crystal.

Heat and tingling sensations like when your arm falls asleep and is only beginning to wake up again. Magic swelled in the air that Aidan hadn't noticed the first time when it was him and Sera touching the crystal. It made everything feel heavy the same way it did when they were in the meadow in the presence of the Enchantress. Did all magic leave you feeling pressed down and smothered? The crystal's light pulsed, and after a few moments, the magic in the air faded.

Leola and Enya dropped their hands from the crystal, rubbing their fingers together. Cedar spoke again, and both girls jumped at the sudden intrusion of actual words into their minds.

"Now that you can understand us, things will be a lot simpler," he declared.

A smaller pink dragon appeared at his side instantly with magic, and Sera wiggled in excitement next to Aidan.

"This is Zelie. She will take you to find some food," Cedar continued.

Zelie was smaller than Harkin, but only slightly. She looked tiny next to Cedar, who towered over all of them. She stepped forward, flapping her wings once before tucking them in tightly to her side.

"Come with me. I'm sure you all are hungry." Zelie's voice was higher and tickled Aidan's ears. He smiled at the sensation and the news. Food had never sounded so good.

"Touch the scales on my chest, and we will be able to travel much faster."

All four of them stepped forward, placing their hands on her pink scales. While Harkin's scales were smooth, almost soft,

Zelie's scales had a sandy texture. She still gave off heat, and Aidan found the sensation soothing now.

The familiar darkness of traveling and the tug of magic filled him with peace instead of fear. He wondered if the others were beginning to feel the same way.

When the light returned, they were standing in a smaller cavern with a large fire burning in a pit at the center. The dragons surely ate their food raw, but here the smell of roasting meat filled the air. Aidan's stomach grumbled in anticipation.

"What is that smell?" Sera asked.

"That is roasted deer. We do not eat cooked meat often, but some of our younger dragons find it easier to chew when they are first hatched." The dragon lifted a claw and dragged out a large stone slab and the large piece of roasted meat cooking on it.

"It will be hot, but I'm sure you'll be able to eat it soon." Zelie prodded the meat with her snout before facing the children again. "I'll be back to see you soon."

She vanished without a sound yet again.

"I guess we should try it, then?" Leola asked.

The others shrugged and followed her to the stone slab. They were filthy, and they had no utensils, but their hunger didn't care. Carefully, they pulled apart pieces of tender meat, blowing on their fingers and cringing at the heat of it, but the first bite to hit their mouths was complete perfection.

Aidan never took his eyes off the food, and there was plenty of it. Each of them ate until they were full, and Sera tugged at Aidan's tunic to show him a stream of water running on the other side of the fire that Leola had found. They knelt and drank their fill, and when they were finally finished and satisfied, they slumped against the far wall and sighed in contentment.

As much as Aidan wanted to be home, he was too tired to get up. Soon, the dancing light of the fire and its warmth, along with his full belly, lulled him into a deep sleep.

Chapter 19

The Gathering

Sera woke up slowly as someone gently nudged her shoulder, whispering her name. She opened her eyes to see Enya mere inches away from her face. She startled backward, only to collide with the stone cavern wall behind her. She winced and rubbed the back of her head.

"Sorry, Sera, are you okay?" Enya frowned.

"Yeah, I'm okay. What's going on?" She asked, scanning the area to find Aidan and Leola standing with Harkin and Zelie.

"The dragons said the league is gathering, and they want to speak with us. We have to go." Enya offered her a hand and tugged Sera to her feet.

She stretched, feeling achy and tired after sleeping on the hard floor. She hoped they would be done soon and could go home. Everything she thought would be brilliant about seeing dragons had proved exhausting. Not to mention the well of dark magic threatening their world.

She and Enya joined Aidan and Leola. The other two reached for Harkin's chest, while Zelie stepped forward for Enya and Seraphina to touch her instead.

Sera wasn't sure she would ever get used to this form of travel. It was over quickly, though, and they found themselves standing in the chamber with the crystal yet again. The same five dragons they had met before stood in front of them again, forming a semi-circle around the crystal.

Lila, the large purple dragon, gazed at them with curious eyes. The chamber was warm and humid, likely due to the dragons gathered within. Enya and Leola appeared nervous and remained frozen in place, noticing the stillness of the others. Dragons didn't seem to be creatures prone to fidgeting.

"We are happy to see that you accomplished your task, small ones. I won't lie; I had my doubts about your ability to succeed. But here you are." The dragon's rough voice grated on Sera's ears.

"Excuse me," Enya held up her hand like she was waiting to be called on in their classes. "We really need to find a way back home to our parents. I don't know how long we slept, or how long we've been gone, but I know they have to be really worried about us."

Lila tilted her head, assessing Enya's statement. "You're right. We need to get you home soon, and we will. But we must explain to you the danger that is coming for our world."

"Danger?" Leola asked.

"Yes, there is a darkness coming because the human king has grown greedy. He is a new ruler, but his thirst for more leads him, not his love for his kingdom or his people," Lila explained.

Sera remembered the coronation celebration their village had held a few months ago. She hadn't paid attention to the conversations the adults had; she enjoyed the festivities of the day, getting lost in the excitement. The food and games, the dancing and music—it had been wonderful, and the most excitement her tiny village had experienced for as long as she had been alive.

"There is a dark sorcerer in this world. He lives in the western mountains, but we believe the king has found him. If the well of darkness is opened, it will give the king absolute power over all creatures—his enemies as well as his people. But it will disturb the balance of the world. Storms will grow more volatile. The whole world will crumble under the weight of it." Lila paused, looking each of them in the eye. "In fact, we believe he has already opened it partially. That's why the storms rage, and the stars awakened."

"What are we supposed to do about it?" Leola asked, and Sera understood how she felt. They were just kids. How could they stop a powerful sorcerer?

"You four have been chosen. You four will be the next dragon riders, and we will work with you to find the sorcerer and destroy the well once and for all. The stars have spoken." Lila finished and let her words sink in.

The stars! Sera remembered the night they had ventured to the cove in the hopes of finding the dragon constellations in the sky. There had been so many! The elders were thrilled, and it was surely a sign. Right after that, they found the egg in the cave.

"The stars *were* important! They were a sign!" Sera exclaimed.

"We do not know why you were chosen, but we know that Jadon does not make mistakes. Harkin will return you to your home, where you can rest. But soon, you will be needed here to plan our next move and to train for what is to come. We will contact you soon."

The words felt heavy and important, and Sera wanted to ask more questions, but she remained quiet. The others kept their thoughts to themselves. Harkin stepped forward, spreading his wings.

"Are you ready to go home, Firestar?"

Aidan nodded in answer and reached forward to place a hand on his chest. Sera wondered why Harkin seemed to only talk to Aidan, and why he called Aidan *Firestar*? She didn't have time to ask. She, Enya, and Leola joined Aidan, and the magic pulled taut on their bodies, transporting them through darkness to home.

Chapter 20

Home

Angry, dark clouds swirled overhead—the stars hidden from view. Wind whistled across the cove, tugging at their clothes and hair. Enya wrapped her arms around herself, bracing against the storm that was brewing the moment they arrived.

A bright flash of lightning lit up the sky, followed quickly by a crack of thunder. The storm would soon release a deluge. The dragon, Harkin, was gone—vanished into thin air on waves of magic.

She opened her mouth to speak when voices reached her from outside the cove near the trails through the forest. The others hunkered together, hiding themselves from the wind and thunder as best they could. Enya grabbed Seraphina's hand, pointing toward the trail before running for the cover of the trees.

Another crack of thunder shook the ground, and the first drops of rain splashed onto her cheeks. Leola and Aidan had followed, but her mind focused on the voices screaming their names in the dark.

"Mom! Dad! We're here!" She screamed.

"Enya?" A lantern shone toward them from the trail, and her mother's face appeared through the shadows. "Enya! Seraphina!" Mari screamed.

It was the best sound in the world. Enya and Seraphina collided with their mother, their father coming up behind her and wrapping all of them in his arms.

"Veda! Milo! They're here!" Their dad yelled over his shoulder.

Leola and Aidan's parents sprinted down the trail, embracing their children, sobs slipping from their mom's lips.

"I'm so sorry, Momma!" Sera cried, "We didn't mean to disappear."

Enya pulled back from her mom and wiped tears from her face. She saw her friends' parents signing quickly, just as emotional as the rest of them.

"What happened? Where did you all go?" Mari asked, but another crack of thunder interrupted her, and the rain turned into a downpour.

"Let's get them home, Mari," their dad shouted over the storm. She nodded, gripping each of her daughters' hands tightly.

They all hurried down the trail, slipping in the mud and flinching with each lightning strike and corresponding rumble of thunder. Enya had never seen a storm this angry, this powerful. She watched the tree tops sway in the breeze, wondering if they would remain standing when the winds finally quieted.

They stumbled into their house, drenched and shivering, but home. Finally, home.

"Take off your clothes and get in front of the fire," their mother commanded. Her voice was tinged with anger and relief.

The girls complied, tossing their filthy, soaked clothes on the ground and standing in just their thin undershirts and bottoms. Their mom ushered them to the fireplace, not worrying about her own clothes, dripping water all over the floor. Their father brought blankets for each of them and wrapped them up tightly.

The warmth of the blankets and the fire provided pure comfort, and the sisters sat cross-legged as close to the flames as they could get without burning themselves.

"What were you thinking!? Leaving the house when the earthquake had just happened!" Their mother threw her hands up, her brow furrowed in frustration. "We told you to stay put."

"Mari," their dad whispered, pressing a steady hand on her shoulder. "Breathe, darling."

"Breathe? Destan, we almost lost them. We did lose them. I can't believe we found you again." Her chest rose and fell quickly, her breath ragged.

Enya felt guilt churn in her stomach. She had never seen her mom look this terrified and angry at the same time. A lot had happened over the past few days, and she didn't know how they would explain it to their parents. Would they even believe the story of how they found a dragon's egg in a cave and were swept into a whirlwind of danger when the dragon carried them away to the mountain? Well, at least it carried Seraphina and Aidan. Leola and Enya ended up dumped in a nightmare.

She wasn't sure she believed it had truly happened. Maybe this was all just a terrible nightmare. Sera stared at the fire, blinking slowly, on the verge of falling asleep right there on the floor.

"Enya, where did you girls go? We told you to stay in the house, especially after the earthquake caused such extensive damage!" Mom was doing her best to control her frustration and fear, but it slipped into her tone regardless.

Enya swallowed, her nerves getting the best of her. "It's going to sound crazy, Mom."

"I think we are past crazy at this moment, baby girl," Dad murmured.

She looked at Sera, awaiting confirmation to continue. Sera nodded, then looked shyly at their parents. Enya wondered for a moment what Aidan and Leola's parents were saying.

"Well, Sera sort of stumbled upon a dragon egg a couple of days ago," Enya started, but her mom held up a hand, closing her eyes.

"I do not want lies, Enya. Only the truth, please."

"But it *is* the truth, Mom! Enya isn't lying! The day of the earthquake, we had all been in the cave close to Aidan and Leola's house when it happened. In that cave was a dragon egg. Or portal. I'm not really sure." Sera paused, her eyes pleading for understanding from her parents, for someone to believe what had happened to them.

Enya reached over and placed a hand on Sera's shoulder, smiling softly. She believed her. Sera could be boisterous and impulsive, but she wasn't a liar, and Enya knew firsthand that the world wasn't what it seemed.

"You were in the cave during the earthquake?" Dad asked, his voice tight.

Enya and Sera nodded.

"Something magical happened, Dad. I promise that we never meant to disappear and worry you. It was a bit out of our control at the time," Enya explained.

Their parents exchanged a glance, so many unspoken words passing between the two of them.

Mom sighed before turning her attention back to her girls. "Okay, tell us everything that happened. From the beginning, please."

The girls smiled at each other and told their parents all that happened with Harkin, the Enchantress, and the League of Dragons.

At first, Enya feared they would be angry, telling them not to lie or talk about such impossible things, but they surprised her. Every outlandish moment, every event that seemed unreasonable, her parents accepted as truth, listening quietly and not interrupting. When they were finished, Mom had her eyes closed, and Dad stared intensely at the fire, his mind elsewhere.

"You believe us, right?" Sera's voice came out small and uncertain.

Dad broke out of his thoughts and smiled softly at Sera. "Of course, we believe you. I don't understand why, after all these centuries, the dragons would reveal themselves to us. We have always believed them to be extinct. Why did they leave?"

Mom opened her eyes and drew in a deep breath. "There was an old story of a people determined to exist outside the natural order of things. They wanted no part in the magic. No part of the power the dragons brought. They feared them, even though they needed them desperately.

"It's a very old story that not many speak about. But their desire to be separate—to be independent of the dragons—made everything shift dangerously. The world has suffered for it ever since. Or so the story goes."

Sera's and Enya's mouths dropped open in shock, while Dad frowned.

"I remember hearing one of the elders speak of this, long ago, when I was a boy. It was one of the older elders who no longer lives this side of the stars."

Mom shared a silent moment with Dad, both lost in memories.

"It's possible the story is true. Maybe the dragons left because they were rejected rather than dying off as we were taught to believe," Mom pondered.

Silence fell over the room again, but this time it felt curious instead of heavy—something positive in the face of the unknown.

Chapter 21

Changes

Aidan was exhausted. After his and Leola's parents had taken them home, they spent a good portion of the night cleaning up, dressing in dry clothes, and recounting what had happened to them. He assumed there were a lot of raised voices, but the passionate way his parents signed demonstrated their anxiety more than anything for him. He broke down and explained exactly what happened with the dragon, what the dragon told them, and their encounter with the other dragons.

Honestly, he wasn't sure they believed him, even though Leola confirmed everything and shared her side of the story as well. His parents were angry and terrified. He didn't blame them. Their children had disappeared shortly after a major earthquake in the middle of a storm and were gone for days. Regardless, they didn't dwell on it.

They ate a light dinner of bread and fruit—his parents too exhausted to cook a large, hot meal after searching for them. It was enough, though, especially with how tired he and Leola were.

When their parents left his room, Leola cracked the door partially, peeking in to find him sitting on his bed.

"Are you okay?" She signed.

"Yes... tired," he answered. "Do you think they believed us?"

She shrugged. "I'm not sure. But it explains everything. Maybe Seraphina and Enya told their parents everything, too, and they can confirm our story."

"I hope so. I don't like letting them down. I don't want them to be mad at us forever."

He rested his hands on either side of his legs and gazed toward the window. Leola tiptoed over and sat next to him, patting his leg with her hand.

"Why do you think Harkin disappeared? Why didn't he reveal himself to everyone?" She asked.

Aidan thought for a moment.

"What if they couldn't see him anyway? Remember when we encountered them after the earthquake, they couldn't see Harkin at all, even though the rest of us could."

A terrible thought burrowed into Aidan's mind at the memory. What if Harkin was gone forever? After all they had been through, he couldn't imagine never seeing the red dragon again.

His worry must have been obvious on his face because Leola reached her arm around him to give him a gentle hug before releasing him.

"If everything the dragons told us is true, then he has to come back. They said they need us. To stop...whatever that was called."

"The well of darkness," he clarified.

"Yes, that. It sounds bad, though. I'm still not sure how we are supposed to stop some evil sorcerer who wants to help a king who wants too much power." She bit her lip, wringing her hands for a moment before forcing them still against her thighs. "Couldn't we get in trouble for saying anything bad about the king?"

"If he's as bad as the dragons say he is, then we can't be quiet just because he is the king. Besides, they have a reason for why they want our help. Didn't they say something about dragon riders?" He asked.

"I'm so tired, I can't remember." She sighed and stretched her neck side to side a couple of times.

"Go to bed. Maybe Mom and Dad will let us see Sera and Enya tomorrow," he signed.

She nodded before saying goodnight and walking out of the room, closing the door quietly behind her.

Aidan got under the covers and lay staring up at his ceiling in the silence that always followed him. Except that wasn't true anymore, was it? He didn't live in silence when he was around the dragons.

An ache settled in his chest as he thought about Harkin and where the dragon was in this moment. He wanted his friend back. He wanted someone to talk to without having to use his hands.

Eventually, sleep tugged him into darkness, and his dreams filled with images of caves, dragons, and magic.

THE ROOM GREW HOTTER as the night stretched on. Aidan tossed and turned, trying to get comfortable and finding that he needed to get out from under his blankets. At one point, he woke with a start, imagining that he had heard something, but he rubbed his eyes, drawing in a deep breath, and reminded himself that he couldn't hear anything.

A short time before dawn, he couldn't take it anymore. He woke up sweating, hands trembling. He climbed out of bed, stumbling toward the door. He needed to find Leola or maybe his mom. Perhaps he was coming down with the sickness that was spreading in their village. He did feel feverish. He turned away from Leola's door, thinking better of going into her room in case he was sick.

Sweat dripped down the sides of his face as he moved along the hallway toward their parents' bedroom. When he reached the door, he fumbled with the knob, probably making more noise than he intended. When the door opened, his mom startled awake at the sudden intrusion.

She might have said something, but it was too dark to see. She reached to the side and struck the flint to light the oil lamp next to the bed. The light forced his eyes closed as it chased away the darkness sitting heavy in the room.

He blinked several times, and when his eyes finally adjusted, he found her standing in front of him, pressing a hand to his forehead.

"Aidan, you're burning up!" She signed. She said something else, and his dad sat up in bed, squinting toward him.

She guided him out of the room and to the kitchen, grabbing a thin rag and plunging it into a bucket of water. Dad handed him a small cup of water, which he guzzled down, realizing how thirsty he was, while Mom pressed the cool cloth onto the back of his neck.

It felt amazing, and exhaustion settled into his body again.

"Does anything else bother you? Does your head hurt or your stomach?" Mom asked.

He shook his head. "No, I'm just tired and really hot. Can we open my bedroom window?"

"Sure," Dad signed, "That will make your room a bit cooler."

They walked back to his room, and Leola stood in her doorway, concern etched into her features. "Is everything okay?" She asked.

"Your brother is on fire. I think he has a fever. You'd better stay in your room. I don't want you catching whatever it is he has." Mom was firm, but Leola furrowed her brow.

"We were together most of the day yesterday. I'm sure we were both exposed to the same things." Leola paused, and Aidan knew what she was thinking—they were together except for when she and Enya had ended up in the control of the Enchantress.

"I'm only tired. It's fine," he answered, hoping what he said was true.

Mom settled him back in bed but kept the blankets off his body this time. "Try to go back to sleep. I'll speak with Mari tomorrow. She'll know what to do."

He nodded, but kept his hands still. She bent down to kiss his forehead before stepping out of the room—his dad closing the door behind her. A cool breeze brushed across his skin, coming from the now open window. He took a deep breath before staring at his fingertips.

He must be going mad because it looked to him like his fingertips were glowing a deep red. He lightly pressed his right pointer finger against his left forearm, hissing in pain when the heat coming from his finger was too much. He'd left an angry red mark on his skin, the same way an ember might leave a burn.

His hands were hot like fire.

Something was not right about this. He thought about getting up and sticking his hands into a bucket of water, but his body felt impossibly heavy, and moving wasn't an option.

Instead, he slipped into a deep sleep, the crackling of flames resonating in his mind the rest of the night.

Chapter 22

Disaster

"Leola! Leola, come here! Hurry!"

Leola jerked awake to the smell of smoke. She started coughing immediately, squinting her eyes against the sting of ash and heat. Someone grabbed her hand, maybe her mom?

"We need to get out of the house!"

She stumbled after them, feeling panic rise in her throat, squeezing and making it hard to breathe. Where were Aidan and Dad? Surely, they escaped already. The heat from the flames grew more intense, and she imagined the fire reaching out with claws for her back.

Shouting broke through her shock, and she and Mom practically fell out the front door into the arms of Dad. She coughed harder with her hands on her knees, desperate to clear her lungs. A small hand rubbed her back in soothing circles.

When she lifted her head, to her relief, she found Aidan staring at her with wide, horror-filled eyes. Dad ran past, carrying a bucket of water, along with a few of the neighbor men. Their mom's warm hands grabbed Leola's face, drawing her eyes upward.

"Are you okay? Can you breathe?" Fear laced every word.

Leola nodded, swallowing and squeezing her eyes shut briefly.

Mom turned to Aidan and signed the same questions. He nodded, but Leola noticed his hands clenched tightly at his sides and the angry red marks along the edges of his fingers. Burns. His skin looked burned.

Together, the three of them watched as the fire consumed their home, the unrelenting flames reaching to the sky despite the men's efforts. A loud crash made them flinch as the roof caved in. Their mom's hands flew to her mouth to stifle a sob, but Leola felt the same ache in her chest. Tears blurred her vision, and she reached for Aidan's hand to hold, but he yanked it away before she could take hold of it.

Confused, her eyes found his. Tears streaked down his cheeks, and anguish marred his usually happy face. He shook his head and faced the house again, or what was left of it.

Dawn arrived, and the pale gray light of the rising sun, barely visible behind the clouds, revealed the extent of the damage. Nothing stopped the flames from consuming every inch of their small home. It was all lost.

"Leola!" Enya ran to them from the trail, followed by Seraphina and their parents.

She turned and let Enya embrace her, sobs breaking free from her throat at the same time. She saw Sera rush to Aidan's side, reaching for him, but he stepped back, shaking his head no. Her brother must be hurt.

Leola pulled back from Enya and turned to Aidan.

"You're hurt, aren't you?" She signed, stepping forward.

Sera's eyes darted between the two of them, but Aidan didn't lift his hands to speak. It was his hands; he burned his hands in the house somehow.

"What happened, Aidan?" Sera asked. Leola felt Enya step up closer behind her.

Their parents were murmuring to each other, watching as the fire slowly grew weaker. No one was paying any attention to the four of them.

"Show me your hands," Leola demanded. Aidan dropped his eyes to his feet, still holding his hands in fists.

She moved closer and lifted his chin with her fingers, ensuring that he saw every word. "Aidan, show...me...your...hands," she exaggerated each sign.

More tears rolled down his cheeks, but he obeyed and turned his hands, palm side up. Sera gasped at the sight, but Leola couldn't move. She was frozen in place, staring at the strange swirls and marks on her brother's skin.

His hands were red, and the marks looked like brands pressed into his palms. The swirls spiraled and twined from the tips of his little fingers to his thumbs, and a few slashing marks crisscrossed near his wrists.

"What did you touch to get those marks?" She asked. It had to be the result of touching a hot object, branding him with the patterns from something in the house.

He shook his head and winced when he lifted his hands, but he forced the words out slowly. The movements of his fingers caused him obvious pain.

"Nothing. Woke up... with them... on me," he answered.

"That doesn't make sense," Sera interrupted.

"Where did they come from? Do you know how the fire started? Were you awake?" Leola tried to control her emotions, but she felt her heart pounding harder, and all she could think about was finding answers.

Aidan frowned, closing his eyes briefly, and when he opened them, she knew what the answer was.

"Me. Fire...came...from... me. I think," he signed, wincing again from the movement.

"That's impossible," Leola murmured, her hands growing sloppy in their response, but he understood her well enough.

She wanted to ask more. She wanted to slip away with her brother and her friends and talk things through. But most of all, she wanted to have a home, a house to run to when all of this became too much.

Instead of saying anything else, she turned to face the remnants of their home, the fire having consumed every last piece of the house. Her parents stood helplessly next to Enya and Seraphina's parents. The other neighbors had grown still as well. All the work and efforts to save the house were for nothing.

Their home was gone, and somehow her brother felt responsible for it.

Chapter 23

When Anger Burns

Sera didn't know what was worse—watching her friends' house burn to ash or the fact that one of them believed they were responsible for the tragedy. The pain on Aidan's face said more than anything his hands could describe. The marks on his palms were painful—this much she could see by the stiff movement of his fingers when he tried to sign and the shine of tears building in his eyes with each word.

Enya stared at his hands, unmoving and shaken by the sight of them. Sera had seen these marks before when they had walked among the dragons at the mountain. The cave with the map burned into the stone walls bore marks similar to these. Her stomach felt heavy as she remembered the warning the dragons had given about the well of darkness.

"Is everyone okay over here?" Mari asked.

Sera met her mother's eyes and felt a lump form in her throat at the tears trickling down her cheeks. Leola stared hard at her brother, a war waging inside her, trying to burst out. Sera saw Aidan shake his head slightly, but Leola ignored his plea.

"Actually, I think Aidan burned his hands in the house."

Anger flashed across Aidan's face, but he smothered it quickly when Mari stepped toward him.

"Oh, Aidan, let me see your hands," she signed.

Sera knew her mother was an accomplished healer, but would she react badly to the symbols? Would she understand what they meant?

Aidan resigned himself to her mother's attention, knowing that he wouldn't be able to hide his pain for long. Mari sucked in a sharp breath at the sight of Aidan's palms. Then, her brow furrowed in confusion. She held his hands in hers with his palms facing the gray sky above. Sera couldn't decide where to look—at Aidan's palms, her mother's concerned gaze, or Leola's defiant glare.

Sera nudged Enya, tilting her head in Leola's direction. Enya took the hint and walked over to her friend, whispering something in her ear. Anger rolled off Leola in waves, and Enya did her best to soothe her.

"Veda! Milo!" Mari called for Leola and Aidan's parents.

"What's wrong? What happened?" Veda asked as she took in the sight of Aidan's burned hands. "Aidan! Why didn't you say anything?"

"Did you touch something in the house?" Milo signed.

Aidan kept his hands still, his expression shuttering at the interrogation from his parents.

"I think it's painful for him to sign," Sera clarified.

Veda put one hand over her mouth, stifling a sob. "Oh, honey, I'm so sorry."

Aidan lifted one shoulder, pretending to be indifferent, but Sera knew he was hurting in more ways than one. Being unable to communicate must be terrifying and deeply frustrating. She looked at Leola, finding her standing there with crossed arms, making no effort to hide her anger. None of the adults noticed, however. They were too focused on Aidan.

"Destan, let's take the children to our house. I can bandage Aidan's hands, and everyone can take a moment to catch their breath," Mari reasoned.

Sera and Enya's dad nodded and placed a firm hand on Sera's back, guiding her to the trail. Enya and Leola followed with Aidan and his mom staying close to Mari.

"I'm going to stay behind. Try to get the rest of the fire completely out before seeing what we need to do next," Milo said.

"I'll be back to help you as soon as I get the rest of them settled," Destan responded.

Sera knew what everyone was thinking. Homes were a necessity in Ebonfore. Storms came frequently, and with all the natural disasters that seemed to be occurring one after another, her friends really needed a shelter over their heads.

The sky above churned with dark gray clouds. Who knew how long the break from the rain would last?

When they arrived home, Sera and Enya took Leola to their room to find a new tunic and pants to wear while their mom worked on Aidan's hands. The scent of healing balm wafted into the loft, and Sera found it calming. Her mom would fix Aidan's hands. Their dads would figure out how to build a new house. Everything would be okay.

They came back out to find Aidan's hands bandaged and his mom explaining the feverish symptoms Aidan had experienced the night before. Hearing the words from Veda made a knot form in Sera's stomach. Did Aidan know the fire was coming, or did something happen to him to cause the fire?

"Girls, get some food and water for our guests."

Leola walked to Aidan's side, but he turned his face away from her, refusing to meet her eye. Enya grabbed three cups and went to their rain barrel just outside the kitchen to fill them. Sera grabbed a loaf of bread and some fruit from the cupboard next to the window that looked out at nothing but dense forest.

Leola and Aidan's mom smiled, "Thank you, dear."

Sera felt awkward and nodded her head shyly. When she went to Leola and Aidan, neither of them accepted the food. She had to do something to break this standoff between the siblings. Enya shared a knowing look with her.

"Come with me," she signed quickly.

She led them to the loft, climbing the ladder quickly. Aidan used his fingertips to balance, protecting his sore hands from the rungs. When they all reached the top and sat cross-legged on the floor, Sera spoke.

"Leola, why are you so mad at Aidan?" She met the older girl's eyes, but she didn't waver.

Tension made Leola's shoulders and back tight, and she had crossed her arms again as soon as they sat down.

Enya chose another tactic. "Do you really think you started the fire, Aidan?" Her hands moved smoothly, and Aidan watched with an impassive gaze until the end.

His eyes filled with sadness more than anger, and he dropped his gaze to his hands resting in his lap. He shrugged as if to say he didn't know.

"His hands are marked with strange swirls. He woke up last night with a fever so bad that Mom and Dad looked more worried than I've ever seen them. Until this morning, that is. It all has to do with that horrid dragon and whatever he thinks we can do for him and his kind." Leola's words rushed out of her mouth, biting and wounding anyone she could.

Aidan frowned before lifting shaky hands. "I didn't ask for this! I had weird dreams. Don't know what happened. My hands... felt like fire... hurt."

Tears streamed down his cheeks again, and he rested his tender hands in his lap once more.

Leola opened her mouth to say something in response, but Sera interrupted. "What did you dream?"

He lifted his hands again, winced, then set them down. It was too much, too painful.

"Did you dream about the dragons? About what they told us?" Enya asked.

He nodded. Sera reached over and touched his arm, feeling warmth under his skin that was hotter than normal.

"You do feel feverish," Sera observed. "Do you feel bad?"

Aidan shook his head no, but he lifted his hands, staring intently at his fingertips. Sera noticed it then as well. His fingertips were glowing a very faint red. Enya elbowed Leola in the ribs, gesturing to Aidan's hands.

His sister's eyes widened, mouth opening in shock.

"I think we'd better get outside," Leola declared, rising to her feet and hurrying to the ladder.

The others followed, and all four ran through the kitchen, out the door into the forest—their moms calling after them.

Chapter 24

Sparks of Flame

"Where are you kids going?" Enya's mother yelled.

She wanted to stop and explain, but the glow on Aidan's fingers sent terror coursing through her body. The four of them stumbled into the dense undergrowth of the forest before coming to a stop near a large maple tree. Enya watched as Aidan held his hands up, the glow intensifying on his skin

"What's going on? You can't just run out of the house like that!" Veda scolded. She and Mari arrived right behind the kids.

"Look, Mom!" Leola yelled, pointing toward Aidan and his glowing hands. "This is not normal!"

"Wha—what is that?" Veda hurried to her son's side with Mari close behind.

Mari placed her fingers gently against the back of Aidan's hands, pulling them away quickly as if they burned her.

"When did this start, Aidan?" Mari asked.

"Right before we ran out of the house," Sera answered.

Sweat beaded on Aidan's forehead now, and Enya could feel heat coming off his body—even the air around them grew warm. Tiny flames sparked across the tips of his fingers.

"Hurry! Put your hands down here," Mari commanded.

She had crouched down at the base of the tree, ripping back layers of moss to reveal cool, damp dirt underneath. Aidan obeyed her and knelt, pressing his hands into the soil. Mari covered the backs of his hands with clumps of dirt, even squeezing some rainwater out of the moss to make it muddier.

Enya took a step back, anxious. She wanted to help Aidan, but she also wanted to scream at her mom to get away from him. The possibility that Aidan had burned down his own house seemed more plausible now.

Aidan's tense shoulders relaxed, and a tiny tendril of steam rose from the ground where his hands pressed. The air cooled considerably, and they collectively sighed in relief at the change around them.

"Are you okay?" Leola asked, stepping cautiously toward their moms and Aidan.

Aidan smiled sadly and nodded. Sera hurried to his side, but Enya didn't miss the look of fear in her mom's eyes when she lifted her gaze to Veda.

"What was that, Mari?" Veda asked.

Mari shook her head. "I don't know. Do you think...?" But she didn't finish her thought. Enya knew what she was thinking. She was thinking that Aidan had accidentally burned the house down.

Veda's pale face drained of blood, and she looked a bit like she was going to be sick. "No. That's not possible."

"It has to do with the dragons," Enya said.

All eyes turned to her, including Aidan's, when he realized she had spoken. "We told you about the dragons last night. We told you everything they said, including the part about being chosen as the next generation of dragon riders," she explained.

"Where are these dragons then? Why haven't they shown themselves?" Mari asked, irritation tainting her voice.

Enya glanced at Sera, who nodded for her to continue.

"I don't think you can see them. At least not yet. When you found us in the cove after the earthquake, a dragon was standing there with us, but you didn't notice him."

"She's telling the truth, Mom," Leola confirmed.

Veda frowned, "Do you think the dragons are bestowing magic on humans once again?" She directed her question to Mari.

Mari turned her face to the treetops, searching for something past the very tips of the branches. The clouds above had calmed to a dull gray instead of the usual dark colors that indicated a storm was imminent.

Enya and Sera's mother murmured three words.

"The dragon stars."

Silence settled over them, and Enya felt the heaviness of the statement in her chest. The dragon stars had been unusually vibrant when they appeared. There had been four dragon star constellations in the sky that night. There were four of them, supposedly chosen by the dragons for the beginning of the tenth era.

"Are you okay now?" Veda asked her son.

Aidan lifted a hand and signed yes. He, Sera, Veda, and Mari rose to their feet. Leola stared at her brother's hands. Enya wasn't sure what emotion she was seeing on her friend's face. Worry? Anger? Maybe even some sadness? She wasn't sure how she would feel if Sera had accidentally burned down their home in the early morning hours.

"We need to get back to the house. We'll see what your fathers have come up with regarding the plan to rebuild our home, and then we need to find the elders. They will know what to do."

The four children exchanged wary looks. The dragons hadn't told them to keep all of this a secret, but would it be possible for the elders of their village to accept them at their word?

Enya reached over and grabbed Leola's hand, smiling at her in a way that she hoped was reassuring. Leola's eyes were distant, but she held onto Enya's hand, and together they followed the others out of the forest and back into the kitchen.

Veda and Mari were whispering to each other, no doubt thinking that they should keep their opinions and thoughts between the adults in the room. Destan and Milo had returned from the remains of the other house and were waiting for them at the kitchen table, cups of rainwater in their hands.

"Where were you all?" Enya's dad asked.

Soot marred both of the men's faces from where they had wiped away sweat at one point with dirty hands.

"We need to talk," Mari answered. She looked at the children. "Alone. Can you all go for a walk to the village center?" She reached into a jar hidden in the cupboard and pulled out a few small coins. "You can even grab a treat or two to share."

She handed the coins to Enya.

"Why are you making us leave? We're a part of this. You need us," Enya argued.

"We're the ones who saw the dragons, Mom. Why can't we stay?" Sera added.

But their mother would not be persuaded. Her eyes darted to the side where Aidan and Leola sat—the former looking exhausted, the latter looking lost.

"Go, do what your mother said. Come straight back when you're done," Dad responded.

Enya and Sera reluctantly led the way out the front of the house. Aidan plodded along behind them, gently pressing a hand to Leola's back to guide her to the door.

The contact snapped Leola out of her reverie, and she jerked away like Aidan had hurt her. Disgust made her face ugly, and Aidan's cheeks flushed pink in embarrassment.

"Don't touch me," Leola snarled, her hands matching her expression in their signs.

Enya saw the pain cross Aidan's face, the anger rolling off Leola's body.

"Leola, be kind! It's not your brother's fault," Veda chided.

"But isn't it?" Leola whirled to face their parents, her hands moving in a mad rush of language. "He's the one who had to touch the egg! He's the one who befriended the dragon. He's the one who burned the house down! We have nothing because of him."

Every word was a jab, and every single one hit its mark. Tears welled up in Aidan's eyes, and he turned, running for the front door. Sera reached for him, but he shoved past her outstretched hand, not slowing down as he fled the house. Sera glanced back for only a moment before taking off after him.

Everything was a disaster.

Chapter 25

When Fire Returns

A idan sprinted down the trail, paying no attention to where he was headed. He couldn't run home because, as Leola had been so kind to point out, he had burned it down. He didn't want to go to the village center, where everyone would be gathered and staring at him with sad, pitying eyes.

He didn't want their pity. He wanted to be alone. The cove would have groups of other children playing or elders teaching lessons. He let the silence engulf him and let his feet carry him wherever they would.

He swiped away the tears from his eyes and paused to catch his breath outside the entrance to the cave where this mess had started. Drawing in a deep breath, he slipped into the shadows and the damp air of the cave. Only a short way in, he found the collapse from the earthquake, and disappointment coiled around his chest, making it hard to breathe.

He closed his eyes, sinking to the cool stone floor, and pleaded with someone, anyone, to see that he didn't intend for anything bad to happen. A hand reached out, tapping his shoulder and startling him.

The weak light outside the cave made it difficult to see, but he knew it was Seraphina the moment he opened his eyes. She didn't sign a word—she only joined him on the floor, leaning her shoulder against his.

A knot formed in his throat, but he swallowed it down, thinking of anything else to keep the tears from coming. Sera sensed his struggle and rested her head on his shoulder, laying one hand gently on top of his.

They didn't hurt as much anymore. The ache of the burns had faded, and the cool mud from the forest floor soothed the heated skin. He turned the hand over that Sera wasn't touching, wiggling his fingers and letting little flecks of dirt fall off. The cloth Mari had used to cover the burns was filthy. Sera reached over, pausing to ask for permission. When he nodded, she gently removed the bandage, unwinding it until it fell away.

The swirls were still there; the strange symbols appeared permanently inked into his palm. He couldn't make out the details well due to the dim light. His thoughts drifted to earlier and how his hands had glowed when the heat from inside him fought to escape. Could he learn to control the fire, or would it consume him and everything he loved instead?

You can, Firestar.

The words entered his mind as clearly as if the dragon stood next to him and Seraphina in the cave. He looked up, expecting to see the red scales of the creature in front of his face, but the only thing in front of him was the gray stone walls on the other side of the cave.

You can control it, Firestar. Try.

Sera nudged his shoulder, giving him a questioning look. He shook his head and focused on his hands. Quickly, he removed the other bandage and stared intensely at his hands, as if he were waiting for something to happen.

He closed his eyes and imagined warmth flooding into his fingertips like warm water. He remembered the way the fire felt on his icy skin the night before, when they rushed into their home after getting soaked from the rain. He pictured the glow of his fingers earlier, before Sera's mom figured out how to stop it. His mind focused on the sensations as if Harkin himself directed his thoughts.

Suddenly, Sera grabbed his arm, jerking hard. He opened his eyes to find his hands glowing a soft reddish light. The air in the cave grew warm, and the dampness of the stone floor and walls faded.

The light intensified, and they squinted against the brightness. Aidan curled his fingers around the light, pretending he held something like a fruit in his hand. The movement shifted the power pulsing off him until tiny flames emerged, a ball of fire forming in his palms. He panted against the strain of pulling the fire out of himself and harnessing it to protect Sera.

She hadn't let go of his arm yet, gripping tightly to him and staring in wonder at the magic flowing from his body. He could see the flames reflected in her dark brown eyes, and he realized that Sera wasn't afraid. No trace of terror could be found in her expression.

Her excitement at seeing this strange power helped to ease his fears about controlling it. He wanted to see what else he might be able to do, but his body felt weak. It took a lot of energy to restrain this much heat, and the cave was growing too warm the longer he held the fire in his hands.

He closed his fingers around the flames. The glow dimmed until it faded completely, plunging them back into the eerie, weak light of the cave entrance.

Sera laughed next to him. He felt her body tremble with excitement, and he could barely make out her smile, but he felt her joy bubbling over from her. This was nothing short of miraculous.

They launched to their feet, tripping over each other as they rushed out of the cave, colliding with Enya and Leola and knocking the older two to the ground.

"I'm sorry!" Sera apologized, helping her sister to her feet first.

The joy of the moment dissolved as quickly as it had come.

Aidan stood back, crossing his arms, his body betraying his true feelings about Leola standing in front of them. His sister stood and dusted her hands off on her tunic. She stared at her feet for a few moments, avoiding Aidan's gaze, but he wasn't going to give in. If she wanted to be here, she could apologize first.

"Come on, guys, can't you apologize and move on? Please?" Sera pleaded.

"Leola, you know Aidan didn't intend for any of this to happen. None of us did, but we're here now, and I don't think we have much of a choice in whether we deal with the dragon situation or not," Enya reasoned.

Aidan felt a twinge of hope in his chest at her words, and he lowered his arms, wondering if Leola would relent. His sister shifted from foot to foot for a moment before meeting his gaze and sighing.

"I'm sorry. I was mad about our house and about the whole Enchantress situation," Leola signed, her lips trembling as she held back a fresh wave of tears. "I hate it. I hate that our home is gone, and we have nowhere to stay. And I hate that the dragons brought us into this mess. That they chose us, whatever that means." She sniffled and lowered her hands.

"I'm sorry that for some reason, I was given this curse, or whatever it is," Aidan began.

"It's not a curse!" Sera objected.

"Sera, be quiet…" Enya attempted to silence her sister.

"No, Enya, I won't let Aidan pretend that what happened to him is something awful. Sure, we didn't ask for the bad parts of our story to happen, but they did, and they don't erase the good parts. You have to see what he can do now! It's amazing!" Sera finished, smiling broadly at Aidan.

"What can you do?" Leola asked, curiosity filling her eyes.

"It will be easier if I show you, I think," Aidan answered.

Leola raised her eyebrows but stayed silent, waiting to see what her brother might do. Aidan's heart pounded; he hoped he would be able to create the fire again, without harming anyone at least.

He held his palms open toward the sky and closed his eyes, imagining the heat and fire that had surged from within him when he created the fireball in the cave with Sera. The air slowly felt warmer around him as sweat formed on his forehead. He opened one eye and found the markings on his palms glowing bright red.

In the cave, the light had been too intense; he and Sera hadn't been able to see the way the spirals came alive with the red light. He kept his focus on his hands and slowly brought the edges of his palms together as if he were scooping water into them to drink. Instead of water, it was light, and the slight movement made the light flare brighter until flames emerged from it.

The effort to contain the fire taxed his body, and he felt his breath coming in short, labored gasps. Sera stepped up beside him and rested a cool hand on his shoulder. The touch grounded him enough that he was able to close his fingers around the flame, extinguishing it in a puff of smoke.

His heart slowed gradually, but the feeling of pure joy at the sight of magic in his hands made his skin feel tingly all over. When they ventured into the cove, he never anticipated everything unfolding the way it did. Magic, real magic, was available to him with a thought. Well, sort of. It was exhausting drawing it out and keeping it under control.

"See! I told you he could do something amazing now." Sera bounced on her toes.

"You look terrible," Leola stated, and Enya elbowed her in the ribs.

Aidan fought the smile pulling at his lips. "I know," he signed.

"It looks hard. I mean, it looks like it's difficult for you to do," Leola pointed out.

"It is. It takes a lot of my energy to draw it out and then to hold it," Aidan paused, looking contrite. "I think I burned the house down. I was so hot, and my hands felt like fire. I think that the magic came out of me without me realizing it when I slept. You were right. It was my fault."

Sadness settled like a weight on Aidan's shoulders. Leola rubbed the back of her neck, then closed the distance between them, embracing him tightly. When she pulled back, she signed silently.

"You didn't do it on purpose, and it wasn't fair for me to blame you the way that I did. I really am sorry about snapping at you."

"I forgive you," Aidan replied.

Sera was about to speak when Aidan heard a strange humming in his ears. He pulled away from Leola, searching for the source of the sound.

"What is it?" Leola asked after she tapped him on the shoulder.

"Do you hear that?" Aidan answered.

She furrowed her brow, and Sera and Enya exchanged a confused glance.

"I don't hear anything. Do you guys hear something?" Leola asked the other two.

Both Enya and Sera shook their heads. How did he hear something when his friends obviously couldn't?

"It's a humming sound. Sort of the way it sounded when the dragons spoke to us before we touched the crystal," he explained.

Together, they moved in a circle, searching the sky for any sign of winged creatures flying overhead. The sound intensified, and Aidan clasped his hands to his ears, wishing it would relent.

A loud crack filled the air, and Aidan knew the others had heard it because all of them jumped and whirled around searching for the source. They stood with their backs together in a circle, facing outward, ready for whatever was coming. With the crack, the humming ceased—the vibrations fading—and Aidan cautiously lowered his hands.

A whoosh of air blew through their hair and tugged at their clothes, followed by a warmth he recognized.

Look up, Firestar.

Aidan tilted his head back and opened his mouth in surprise as Harkin descended from the sky directly above the four of them. The dragon had returned.

Chapter 26

Dragon Fire

They scattered apart, making room for the red dragon to land where they had been standing moments before. The wind from Harkin's wings rustled their hair and clothes and chilled them each in turn. Leola placed her hands on her hips, bracing for whatever message the dragon was bringing this time.

The creature landed gracefully, his claws digging into the soft earth like he relished the cool feel of the dirt beneath him. Though Leola wanted to trust the dragon, he terrified her, and all she could envision was those sharp teeth biting into her.

Silence settled among them, but Leola had the feeling Harkin was speaking to Aidan in his mind. She felt a tiny spark of anger toward the dragon but quickly suppressed it. Something had been put into motion by someone far more powerful than any of them, and not even the dragon was responsible for it.

Aidan nodded slowly, pondering whatever Harkin was telling him. After a few more moments of strained silence, Harkin spoke to the rest of them.

It felt strange to hear the vibrations in the air and understand them. Leola hoped it would become less weird the more they were exposed to it.

"It has come to our attention that Aidan's gift has revealed itself," Harkin declared. "A most powerful gift indeed."

"You're talking about the fire?" Sera asked, her expression lighting up like it was the morning of the winter solstice.

"Yes, I'm talking about the fire. Each dragon rider obtains a gift connected to their bonded dragon." Harkin turned his head to Aidan and blew a puff of red-tinted smoke into the air.

"Are you saying... that I am your dragon rider?" Aidan signed in wonder.

Sera bounced on her toes, squealing in excitement. "I told you it wasn't a bad thing!"

"What does that mean for the rest of us?" Enya inquired.

Leola envied her friend's ability to think logically about any situation. She was still coming to terms with their house being gone, and now the others seemed to be moving on, celebrating this discovery.

"Each of you will be bonded to a dragon. I don't know who your *copanias* are, but they will reveal themselves when the time comes." Harkin stretched his wings, beating the air a couple of times before tucking them into his side.

Leola opened her mouth to ask a question when a scream ripped through the air around them. All four of them spun to face the path leading to the village center. A small girl who looked to be a few years younger than Aidan and Sera pointed toward them, terror filling her face. The girl's mother ran to her side, scooping her into her arms and asking what was wrong.

"We need to go. Now!" Leola commanded.

No one argued with that, and all four of them took off in the opposite direction, searching for the trail that would lead to the cove. Harkin took flight and soon vanished into the low-hanging clouds overhead.

Leola charged ahead and took a sharp turn onto a tiny deer path just to the right of the trail. The branches scratched at their faces and snagged in their tunics, but they didn't slow down. She knew this path was a shortcut to the cove—one the deer used frequently enough to make it mostly clear of obstacles.

She skidded to a stop when they emerged into the clearing, Aidan bumping into her before steadying her with his hands on her arms.

"Did the girl's mother see Harkin?" Leola asked, trying to catch her breath.

She hadn't been able to see from where she stood. The girl had definitely spotted the dragon, but was he still invisible to the adults around them? She hoped so.

"I don't know. She might have missed him when she picked up her daughter." Enya didn't sound certain, which made Leola nervous.

"The elders wouldn't be against Harkin, would they? He's not a danger to any of us." Sera looked back and forth between Enya and Leola, hoping they had an answer she wanted to hear.

"He *is* a dragon, and most of the elders don't believe dragons exist anymore. How do you explain something that people thought was extinct for years?" Leola argued.

"Sera is right, though. Harkin is here to help us," Aidan interjected.

"Regardless, we need to hear what the elders think." Enya grimaced at the expression on her younger sister's face. "I'm sorry, but it's true. I think our parents are consulting the elders today anyway. They're worried about those marks on Aidan. They saw the sparks and felt the heat."

Leola nodded and grabbed hold of Aidan's hand. "It'll be okay. We'll tell them what the dragons told us."

Aidan looked skeptical; then the same contemplative expression fixed itself on his face. Leola knew Harkin was speaking to him. Moments later, the sound of the dragon's wings beating the air echoed around them as he landed quietly in the grass.

"Harkin, you said something about each of us being bonded to a dragon? What did you call it?" Leola asked.

"*Copanias*. Your bonded dragon is called your *copania*. That is the way of the dragon riders. We don't know who will bond. It is simply the way of Jadon," Harkin spoke the words with reverence for the god of their world.

Leola felt goosebumps prickle on her skin at the name. Could they really have been chosen to aid in the rescue of their home? Why would Jadon want to use them? They were just kids.

Harkin shifted his gaze to Leola as if he'd heard her thoughts, as if he knew what her doubts were. He stared at her, neither impatient nor annoyed, waiting for her to voice something. She couldn't explain how she knew this, but she felt it in her chest and deep in her belly. The others sensed the gravity of the moment, understanding that a silent conversation was happening between the dragon and Leola.

She couldn't hold her thoughts in a moment longer. "Why us? We're just kids," she whispered, her hands moving slowly.

"Children believe. They are not afraid of the impossible. Not unless someone tells them to be afraid. Children are always the first to see us, and sometimes, they are the only ones who do."

The words seeped into each of them, taking root in their hearts and minds. Leola found them difficult to swallow. She hadn't believed, hadn't wanted to face the truth surrounding the events interrupting their normal lives, but she couldn't deny it either.

"Aidan has firepower?" Sera asked.

"Yes, dragon fire is shared between him and me. He will have to learn to control it, and that, in itself, won't be easy."

"How do I learn to use it? I don't want to burn anything else down." Aidan signed urgently.

"We will train soon. But first, you must rest longer and wait for the League to send the other dragons awakened by the choosing."

"What's the choosing?" Enya inquired.

"It's what has already happened. The night of the dragon stars, four constellations appeared—a most rare and unusual occurrence. Jadon put into motion the awakening of dragons bonded to the four chosen dragon riders. You were chosen that very night, and soon you will meet the dragons chosen to be your partners." Harkin snorted a plume of smoke, a look of satisfaction on his scaly, red face.

Leola observed her friends and her brother. This was a lot to take in, especially the revelation that not only Aidan but the rest of them as well would be gifted with magical powers. How would they explain that to their parents?

She sighed, about to remind them they needed to get to the village square to buy the treats their parents had sent them off to get, when she heard voices calling their names.

"Sounds like our parents are looking for us again," Enya responded.

"We'd better find them. I'm sure they're tired of worrying about us at this point," Leola declared.

Harkin yawned before launching into the sky and flying away. Aidan watched him with curiosity, intrigued by the dragon's words.

"Come on, let's get to the trail." Leola led the way out of the cove toward the main path that meandered through the forest amongst the homes in Ebonfore.

Chapter 27

The Elders

Their moms found them as they worked their way up the trail toward Sera and Enya's home. Sera felt giddy after everything Harkin had revealed to them. She wanted to find her dragon and learn what gift might be placed on her when her bonded arrived. She did not want to face the frustration and worry evident on her parents' faces when they met them on the trail.

"There you are. Where did you run off to?" Mom asked.

"Leola and I found them near the cave, but everything is okay now," Enya answered, giving a knowing look to Leola.

Veda sighed, "We need you to stay with us now. We're going to meet with the elders to discuss what's happened. Your fathers are already with them to see if they are all available to speak. We need to see what they think about the markings on your hands, Aidan."

Aidan glanced down, and Sera's gaze followed his. She thought the markings were beautiful, and now that she knew they were connected to his firepower, they filled her with hope.

"Do we have to meet with them?" Aidan signed.

"Yes, we need to. They will understand what's happening better than we do," said Veda.

"Come along, we can start heading over there. I'm sure they will be willing to make time for us today." Mom nudged

Sera and Enya gently on the back, and they continued up the trail toward the village center.

News of the dragon sighting had spread quickly. Excited chatter filled the air, and people spoke animatedly at various vendors. The closer they got, the clearer the conversations became.

"Do you think she really saw a dragon?"

"No! Dragons are extinct. They have been for generations."

"I heard she saw two of them."

"She's just a small child. What does she know?"

"Children are quick to spy the unusual, though. It's a gift of theirs."

The words mingled and blended, a chorus of doubt and wonder all around them. The village center consisted of ten permanent vendors in a circle around a small wooden building. The wooden structure was the center for studies and commerce. Some larger villages housed their schools in a separate building, but Ebonfore was small enough that all official procedures were done in one place. Studies for children during the fall and winter seasons. Regular discussions on bartering, market activity, and trade among their neighboring villages, the rest of the time.

This was the heart of Ebonfore, and Sera normally loved the hustle and bustle that filled the area during the peak market days. Today, however, she felt nervous—afraid of what the elders might say when they gathered in the center structure.

Their Mom and Veda led the way past the excited villagers into the building, where Destan and Milo stood speaking with the five elders. It occurred to Sera that this situation felt strangely familiar. The League of Dragons had consisted of five great beasts who seemed to hold all the knowledge of the world in their minds. Now, the five elders cast glances in the direction of the children, specifically Aidan.

Sera felt Aidan falter next to her, and she did the only thing she could at the moment—grasp his hand and hold on tight.

"I hope I'm right in assuming you'll hear our concerns?" Veda asked the primary elder, James.

"You're correct. We are intrigued by the stories your husbands bring to us. Please, come sit."

Elder James gestured to several cushions spread around on the floor in a circle. He and the other elders took their places on five large ones, while they and their parents found additional pillows to sit on.

"You said your children encountered dragons a few nights ago after the dragon star constellations filled the sky. We would like to hear from them." Elder James focused his attention on Aidan, and Sera watched her friend swallow nervously.

"We won't rush you, but let's not delay telling the full story. Aidan, begin," Elder Agatha signed.

Aidan's cheeks flushed, and he wiped his hands on his pants, looking as nervous as Sera felt. She touched his forearm, then nodded encouragingly to him.

Aidan proceeded to explain everything they had experienced, from the dragon stars to the cave encounter with the dragon egg. He told the tale of being taken to Dragon Mountain and losing Enya and Leola, who jumped in, confirming his account of the story.

He explained what the dragons said about the dark sorcerer and the new king's reliance on him for power he did not deserve. He finished by saying the dragons revealed that he and the others were dragon riders waiting to be bonded to their dragons.

The elders kept their thoughts to themselves the entire time he signed. No one interrupted or rushed him; no one asked questions. He let out a long sigh when he finished, resting his hands on his thighs.

The five elders exchanged glances, and Sera wasn't sure what she saw on their faces. Curiosity? Doubt? A little of both? Finally, an ancient-looking woman, permanently hunched and with eyes of deep gold, lifted her gnarled hands to sign.

"We have waited for generations for the dragons to rise again. The stars do not lie. Jadon has chosen."

She moved slowly, forming each word with painstaking care, before folding her hands in her lap again. The other elders remained silent, pondering her words. After a few more minutes, Elder James spoke.

"Elder Sage speaks the truth. We have always known there would come a day when evil would rise to destroy what is good. There have been murmurings about the possibility that the dragons did not die, but rather, they vanished from our sight," he paused, contemplating his next words carefully. "This well of darkness is...a disturbing development."

"How do we know the children encountered actual dragons and not a deception left for them by the sorcerer?" Elder Conrad interjected. He was a wiry, middle-aged man who made them write and rewrite their history lessons repeatedly during their study sessions.

Sera knew she shouldn't dislike the man, but she was not very fond of him either.

"The proof is marked into the boy's flesh, Elder Conrad," Elder Andra remarked, her voice scratchy and her sign language choppy.

"A sorcerer could accomplish the same thing. We must be cautious before making any decisions. It is heresy to question the king. Do we really believe he would choose dark magic to rule his kingdom?" Elder Conrad's voice rose in volume and annoyance with every word, but Sera understood the underlying emotion he was trying to suppress—fear.

"You know as well as I do, Conrad, that humans have always struggled with reining in our desire for more. The king is no different from you or me," Elder James declared.

Suddenly, the oldest elder, Elder Sage, rose to her feet, grasping her staff tightly and leaning most of her weight on it. When she gained her balance, she leaned her staff against her side and lifted her hands again. The others fell silent. The elder captivated Sera; she imagined the woman knew the secrets of Endeilo—the universe in which all worlds exist, interconnected—in her soul. Maybe she even spoke with Jadon face-to-face.

"The dragons will come soon. We must inform the village, or people will panic. You fear the king too much, Conrad. No ruler should reign undisputed. No ruler should think they deserve unquestioned power. There must be a balance, and the dragons will bring balance to the world again."

Elder Conrad huffed and crossed his arms. The other elders nodded their agreement with the eldest, and Sera felt hope surge through her body again. She turned to Aidan, smiling, and he returned it with a soft one of his own.

Everything would be all right. They simply needed to wait...

CRACK!

The walls of the building shook, jolting her from her thoughts. Their parents jumped to their feet, and Sera saw her dad run to help Elder Sage, who had been knocked off balance and dropped to one knee, clinging to her staff.

Another loud boom echoed outside, and they all ran from the building to see what was causing the commotion. Screams filled the air as another loud crack resounded, and one of the vendor stalls collapsed. Sera searched the village center for the cause of the commotion, but nothing was visible other than a blackening sky and angry clouds swirling overhead.

A blinding streak of lightning stretched across the sky like an angry claw, and another boom followed almost simultaneously. The lightning reached down again and struck another vendor stall—this one erupting into flame.

This was no ordinary storm.

Chapter 28

Firestar

"We need to get back home! Everyone, go to our house!" Destan yelled over the sound of the wind whipping through the trees.

Enya shoved Leola toward the trail after Aidan and Seraphina, disrupting her friend's shock at the sight of the storm overhead. They raced after their siblings, their parents close behind as far as she could tell.

The wind howled through the trees, and limbs snapped from the force of its wrath. This storm was even worse than the storm they'd experienced a few days ago when Harkin stole them away, and it seemed to come with no warning. Her heart pounded, and she did her best to stay on her feet as the rain fell.

The path grew sloppy and slick, and she stumbled more than once. Aidan and Sera were barely visible ahead on the trail; the rain falling so hard it turned the air a misty white all around them. Leola reached back for her hand, attempting to keep them both on their feet.

When they arrived at her house, Aidan and Sera ushered them inside, and their moms slipped in last, slamming the door with enough force that the window rattled.

"Where's Dad?" Enya asked, her voice coming out hoarse and harsh.

"They both went back to help the vendors in the square," Mom answered.

"Those two. They always have to help when they see a need," Veda shook her head.

"Come over here. I'll get the fire started so you can warm up and dry off." Mari moved across the room toward the hearth, but Aidan stepped in front of her and held up a hand, signaling for her to wait a moment.

Then, Enya and the others watched as Aidan closed his eyes, held his hands toward the hearth and the partially burned wood inside. Heat flooded the room, coming from Aidan himself, but she couldn't see any fire yet. She, Leola, and Sera all stepped closer, mesmerized by the glowing symbols on his hands. A few moments later, the tiniest spark of a flame ignited, and he slowly knelt on one knee, stretching his hand out toward the logs and setting the flame on top of them as carefully as if it were a delicate creature.

Maybe it was.

A normal flame of that size would have done little to ignite the logs, but this wasn't ordinary fire. It was magical, and the logs responded by catching quickly. Aidan sighed and clapped his hands together before shaking them slightly, like he was trying to cool them.

The room warmed instantly, and Veda and Mari carefully added a few more logs to the fire to keep it burning strong. They huddled around the hearth, letting the flames dry their clothes.

Enya turned her head to Aidan, marveling at what he had just done. Leola's face expressed the same awe. Perhaps she would learn to be happy about her brother's magic and not resent it. Which reminded her—it wasn't only Aidan who was to be bonded to a dragon, but all four of them had been chosen. To be chosen meant they were to receive powers from their dragons, and for the first time, a part of Enya felt giddy at the idea.

As long as she didn't get a power that would destroy their home.

"What are we going to do about our house?" Leola's question to Veda jolted Enya out of her thoughts.

"Your father spoke with several of the neighbors, and they should be able to build a basic framework with a roof within a day. If this storm lets up, that is."

They all looked at the ceiling when another crack of thunder vibrated the walls. Enya prayed their home would be spared from the lightning striking all around.

Their moms stood for a little longer near the fire before moving to the kitchen to prepare some lunch. Enya turned her attention to Aidan when they left the room.

"What does it feel like to use your power?" She signed.

His mouth curled up in thought before he answered. "It's very hot."

They all burst out laughing at the simplicity of his statement. He waved his arms, trying to draw their attention again.

"What?! It's true. It gets really hot, to the point I think my skin might burn. And I have to concentrate really hard to get the flame to emerge. I hope it's not always this hard," he finished.

"I wonder if you practice, it will get better," Sera pondered.

"Maybe you need the dragon to be close by for it to be easier," Leola stated matter-of-factly.

Aidan's brow furrowed. "You could be right. I haven't really had a chance to practice with Harkin close by."

"It would make sense for that to be true. We're supposed to be bonded to these dragons. It's their power that is gifted to us. Harkin gave you dragon fire; so, he probably needs to be close by for you to use it more effortlessly," Enya said.

"I can't wait to meet my dragon!" Sera exclaimed.

Enya rolled her eyes, and Leola gave her a knowing look. Secretly, she wanted to know who her dragon was, too, and what gift they would give her. But she wasn't going to tell her little sister that. Let Sera be the extravagant dreamer of the two of them. One of them had to be reasonable.

"Honestly, I kind of want to know too," Leola remarked, sheepishly.

It surprised Enya, but she found it comforting to know that her friend was growing more curious about the situation rather than staying angry.

"Harkin calls you Firestar. I hope I get a cool name, too!" Sera smiled, dancing around in front of the fire.

"I hope you get a really interesting name. Like Laughing Star," Aidan teased.

"Hey!" Sera pretended to be offended, but her smile never wavered.

Lunch consisted of more bread, fruit, and some salted goat meat. They ate until they were satisfied, and then the four of them ventured to the loft while their moms anxiously looked out the front windows for any sign of their dads.

Hours later, the storm died out, and the door swung open, revealing Destan and Milo, soaked to the bone and covered in mud.

A house had fallen, and the men had worked hard to get everyone out, including two small children. Mari was needed for her healing knowledge, and after she ensured the other two were uninjured, she gathered a few supplies from the kitchen and rushed out the door.

Muddy boots were discarded, and Destan led Milo to the other bedroom to fetch clean, dry clothes for both of them to change into. When they came out, the exhaustion on their faces made them look even more haggard. Veda bustled back and forth, taking their muddy clothes to the back of the house and getting them food and water to drink.

"Do you think the storm is because of the well of darkness?" Sera whispered, her hands moving quickly.

"It was a strange storm. And really violent," Aidan agreed.

"I think it's all connected. The dragons said everything would get worse. This is definitely worse," Enya paused. "I think we can expect a lot of bad things if the sorcerer isn't stopped soon."

No one spoke after that, but as darkness fell, the sky cleared and the first pinpricks of stars appeared. Four dragon constellations formed, glowing brighter than before, though no one was looking up to see them tonight.

Chapter 29

The Dragon Star Chronicles

The next few days, Aidan heard nothing from Harkin. No whispers in his mind. No random comments on his firepower. He and his family had been staying at Enya and Seraphina's house, and tensions were running high among the kids. He practiced starting the fire every day, and it was getting a bit easier. It didn't feel like enough, though, and when were they going to hear about the other bonded dragons?

No storms came through after the previous one, but no work could begin on their house until others' homes were repaired and even rebuilt. However, today, everyone's efforts were going to his home. Dad and Destan left early that morning and would be gone all day, raising the outer walls and the roof. In a couple of days, they'd be able to move back in.

A tap on the shoulder startled him, but he smiled when he found Sera's bright eyes staring at him.

"Whatcha doin'?" She asked.

He hesitated a moment before answering. "I was thinking about the dragons and wondering why they haven't come yet."

She frowned and turned her gaze to the forest that almost reached into the house. "They'll come. When the time is right, they'll arrive."

"Your signing is getting better," he said.

She giggled before sitting on a log at the edge of the trees. "Thanks. You living here has given me lots more practice."

He walked over and sat beside her, and together they stared at the trees, waiting for something.

"Do you think the king and the sorcerer will ruin all of it?" Her shoulders lifted in a sigh, and he saw tears forming in her eyes.

"I don't know. We have to believe that good will win, right?" He tried to smile, but he understood her fears.

The forest was their home, and the recent events threatened them all. The fabric of their world was in danger of collapse, according to the dragons. He didn't want to believe the dragons at first, didn't want to accept that something terrible was coming for them. But the storms, the earthquakes—everything pointed to something dark coming.

Firestar, it is time. Tonight, at the first star in the sky, meet us where it began.

Aidan stiffened at the voice, having become used to the silence he'd been living with for the past few days. Sera nudged him, her face full of concern.

"What's wrong?" She asked.

"Harkin spoke to me. I think we're meeting the other dragons tonight."

"What? Where!? What did he say?" She stood abruptly, ready to venture off this minute to meet the dragons.

He grabbed the hem of her tunic and tugged.

"Tonight. He said it was time and that tonight at the first star in the sky, we are to meet where it began?" He felt confused by this last part.

They couldn't meet in the cave with the entrance blocked because of the collapse. How were they supposed to get to where they found the egg?

Sera tapped her chin, deep in thought. She must be thinking the same thing he was. Suddenly, her mouth opened in a gasp, and she latched onto his shoulders with a bruising grip.

"Aidan! I know where it began. It wasn't the cave. It was the cove where we saw the very first dragon constellations that night. Remember, there were four of them? And Cedar said we were chosen because the stars had spoken. That has to be what he means. The cove is plenty big enough for dragons to land in."

She was practically vibrating with excitement now. Aidan lifted his hands to say something, but she vanished into the house. He had no doubts that she was searching for Enya and Leola.

He stared into the forest, watching the shadows shift and change with every breeze. The sky was clear today, giving them an unusual picture of blue instead of the normal gray expanse. Stars would be easily spotted in the cove tonight. He hoped not as many people would venture to stargaze as the last time.

WHEN TWILIGHT FELL over the land, the four children ventured out of the house and onto the trails. They had eaten dinner and explained to their parents that they wanted to go to the cove tonight to see the stars. Reluctantly, their parents conceded but reminded them to return home at a decent hour.

This time, Aidan carried a small lantern with them to light the way. The moons were dark tonight, and they didn't want to be left completely unprepared for what might come.

"What do you think we'll find?" Leola asked.

"I think—and maybe see—dragons," Enya suggested, but Aidan couldn't understand her hands well enough as they moved in and out of the lantern light.

He took a deep breath, stepped past the older two, and focused his attention on the path ahead, the trees stretching overhead like great sentinels. If the trees were guarding the secrets of the cove, he hoped they would protect him and the others, too.

The path curved, and he followed it until another trail opened to the side. Stepping through, they found the cove empty, only a slight breeze disturbing the tall grass that blanketed the ground.

"Where is everybody? I thought they would come with the sky so clear," Sera observed.

She intentionally positioned herself in the lantern light for Aidan to understand her. Enya followed her lead and inched closer until all of them were cast in golden light.

"I think everyone is still recovering from the storm and the destruction it caused. People are too tired to come out here," Leola stated.

The sun's last rays blinked out, and the darkness became more absolute. Aidan looked to the sky, marveling at what gazed down at them from above. Sera, Enya, and Leola mimicked him, and he knew without hearing them that the others had gasped at the sight.

The sky was bright with stars, but four constellations stood out, brighter than the rest, glowing a brilliant red. Four constellations in the form of four dragons meant for four children chosen by the God, Jadon.

Aidan dragged his eyes from the stars and watched his friends and sister. Their faces were full of wonder—Sera's practically bubbling with joy, Enya and Leola both appearing awestruck. He was about to touch Sera's arm when a voice burst through the silence in his mind.

Firestar, we have come.

Suddenly, bright flashes of light—all different colors—burst before them. When the flares vanished, four dragons stood, still as statues.

All four were about the same size. Harkin stepped forward first, followed by a green one whose color was like that of the pine trees. Another dragon stepped forward, this one as rich a blue as the lilies they had walked among when confronting the Enchantress. Finally, a dragon whose color reminded Aidan of the deep indigo sky at the first traces of twilight on clear days, joined the other three.

"We have come that you may complete your bonds with us," Harkin declared, his voice almost a growl.

A strange burst of tingles erupted in Aidan's chest. He looked around to find the other three pressing trembling hands to their hearts, experiencing the same bizarre sensation. Something tightened in his chest like a rope, tugging gently on him. Harkin stepped closer, and the tether grew taut. The bond was solidifying between him and the red dragon.

The other dragons stepped toward their respective humans—the blue one toward Leola, the green one toward

Seraphina, and the indigo one toward Enya. The dragons themselves seemed to glow a version of the colors of their scales. Harkin's great head focused on the others, and Aidan found himself doing the same thing.

Sera reached a tentative hand to the green dragon; then she burst out giggling when the dragon pressed its snout into her hand.

Enya stood, wringing her hands together, maintaining eye contact but looking terrified. Her indigo dragon nudged her chest gently, and relief flooded her face.

Finally, Leola stood, arms stiff at her side, and watched as the blue dragon stared at her with skepticism, then resolve. It moved closer, pivoted, and stood shoulder to shoulder with his sister.

Harkin's voice hummed over the cove. "You have met your bonded partners. Leola—this is Coral, and she will give you the gift of water." The blue dragon lifted her head higher, proud of her name and her gift.

"Enya, Rai is your dragon, and she will give the gift of storms." The indigo dragon's eyes flashed with what Aidan thought might be lightning itself.

"Finally, Seraphina, your dragon is Riti. She will give you the gift of foresight. You will see all that could happen, though you might not know the outcome of what actually comes to pass."

The air sparked with anticipation and excitement. Aidan took in the sight of the dragons and their new riders, and he thought maybe, just maybe, they would be able to do something good for this world. The rope tying him and Harkin felt real enough to touch. The buzz of magic beneath his skin grew stronger, and he thought the others were right. Having the dragons near would help them with their powers.

Aidan set the lantern down and reached up to touch Harkin's shoulder. The dragon's warmth seeped into his hand, and he held the other hand up, imagining flames. Instantly, they appeared without much effort on his part.

He laughed at the sight, then beamed even wider when he saw Sera fly overhead on the back of Riti. Soon, the others joined her, and Harkin lowered his head, giving him a knowing look before lowering himself on one scaly leg.

Aidan moved quickly around Harkin's side and climbed up, resting his hands on the dragon's neck. He squeezed with his knees as the creature launched into the air, chasing after the other three.

Today, they would enjoy the flight. Tomorrow, they would begin their training to use their gifts. After that, he hoped—no, he knew they would be ready to face the sorcerer and the wicked king.

The dragon stars glittered above them as the earth fell away. They were chosen. It would all work in the end. Aidan believed that it would.

The End

Acknowledgements

I want to begin by saying thank you to my friend, Cheryl, for acting as my sensitivity/beta reader for this story. Her insights helped me tweak a few areas that I felt could portray my characters better.

Some details of this story came from my daughters' input, as well as their friends, such as the colors each character sees with the egg at the beginning and what colors the dragons are for each character at the end. My daughters also contributed names in some places and helped choose the powers each child received from the dragons.

Special thank you to Eliora Humphrey, who helped design and illustrate the cover for this book.

Thank you to my husband for being patient and continually asking if I was still writing another book.

I hope you enjoy *Firestar* and all that is to come with this four-book series I have planned.

Welcome to the Kingdom of Kida and the Dragon Star Chronicles.

About the Author

Hi! I'm Olivia, and I have had a deep love of reading and all things books pretty much my entire life. I grew up on fantasy and magic, and the fact that I get to write stories full of those things boggles my mind. I hope to continue to grow as a writer and reader every year. I love a variety of genres and consume a diverse range of books. I was born and raised in Kentucky, and I spend a lot of my time outside with my family, enjoying our garden and nature. My horses, cats, and dog also hold a dear place in my heart. Thank you to every person who takes a chance on my book. I hope you like it, and even if you didn't, I'm still grateful you tried it out!

Happy Reading!